ANGE

Nurse Olivia Paine, looking after her neurotic actress cousin in the South of France, is delighted when Dr Morgan Beauclerc shows a special interest in her difficult patient. The admiration of such an attractive man is, she feels, the best possible medicine for Celeste. But to find *herself* falling victim to his treatment is the last thing she expected.

Books you will enjoy
in our Doctor–Nurse series

DR HARTNELL'S DISCOVERY by Elizabeth Petty
TALISMAN FOR A SURGEON by Lisa Cooper
THE PURSUIT OF DR LLOYD by Marjorie Norrell
SISTER STEWART'S DILEMMA by Meg Wisgate
NURSE ON TRIAL by Clare Lavenham
THE UNCERTAIN HEART by Sheila Douglas
NEW CALEDONIAN NURSE by Lilian Darcy
LEGACY OF LOVE by Hazel Fisher
THE MAGIC OF LIVING by Betty Neels
A CANDLE IN THE DARK by Grace Read
DECISION FOR A NURSE by Jean Evans
SISTER MARGARITA by Alex Stuart
HOSPITAL ACROSS THE BRIDGE by Lisa Cooper
BACHELOR DOCTOR by Sonia Deane
NEW SURGEON AT ST LUCIAN'S by Elizabeth Houghton
THE SURGEON'S WIFE by Judith Worthy
DOCTORS DON'T CRY by Elizabeth Gilzean

ANGEL IN PARADISE

BY

LINDSAY HICKS

MILLS & BOON LIMITED
London · Sydney · Toronto

First published in Great Britain 1983
by Mills & Boon Limited, 15–16 Brook's Mews,
London W1A 1DR

ISBN 0 263 74178 8

03/0183

Set in 10 on 12 pt Linotron Times

Photoset by Rowland Phototypesetting Ltd
Bury St Edmunds, Suffolk
Made and printed in Great Britain by
Richard Clay (The Chaucer Press) Ltd
Bungay, Suffolk

CHAPTER ONE

OLIVIA's first impressions of Dr Morgan Beauclerc were not favourable. *Arrogant*, she thought. *Attractive and knows it!*

He walked into the luxuriously furnished room to meet his patient like an actor expecting applause, she thought. Tall, broad-shouldered and narrow-hipped, dark of hair and eyes, very sure of himself and much too handsome in the expensively-tailored dark suit, it was obvious why he had been so highly recommended by Lucy Bellamy when she offered her villa on the Côte d'Azur for the summer.

He smiled with a practised charm, Olivia decided with swift and unreasonable dislike. And Celeste, eyes dark-ringed and too bright in a pale but perfect face, visibly responded to the undeniable magnetism of that smile.

'Well, Mrs Knight,' he said in a deep and very attractive drawl that would quicken any woman's pulse if she felt well enough to take notice. 'How are you feeling after the journey? Not too tired, I hope?'

He did not even glance at the dutifully hovering Olivia who had prepared for his call by putting on her mauve uniform frock and pinning her badge prominently on her breast so that this French doctor would know that he was dealing with a Kit's nurse and treat her with due respect. She was very proud of having trained at St Christopher's, the famous teaching hospital in London whose nurses were sought after throughout the world. Dr

Beauclerc would certainly know that he could expect the very best nursing care for his new patient from a Kit's nurse.

He did not appear to be very French despite his surname, she thought curiously. He had Gallic looks, black curly hair and piercing dark eyes and a very sensual mouth, but he spoke faultless English with a trace of Welsh accent that was intriguing. At the very back of Olivia's mind was the thought that she knew something specific about this doctor with the unusual name. Recollection would probably come to her in the middle of the night . . .

'Utterly exhausted, I'm afraid,' Celeste declared in the lovely, lilting voice that was such an asset for an actress. She held out a slender hand, diamonds sparkling in the sunlight that filtered into the room through the long windows, and bestowed on him the golden smile that had captivated audiences on both sides of the Atlantic—and too many men. 'So silly to be as weak as a kitten after the least exertion . . .' Her beautiful voice trailed off to prove her exhaustion.

She was as enchanting as a kitten but she had claws and could use them, Olivia thought with all the candour of a cousin, observing that an immediate attraction had sparked between the handsome doctor and the very lovely Celeste. What better tonic for any convalescent woman than the admiration and interest of such an attractive man? It was just the kind of medicine to suit Celeste!

'But you were under a great deal of strain for some time before your illness, I understand,' he said, warm and reassuring, very soothing. 'It takes time and rest and a lot of care and understanding to restore someone to good health after a nervous collapse such as you have experienced.'

Hysterics and tantrums, Olivia amended silently. Celeste had used them to get her own way since she was a child. But recently they had been symptomatic of the disturbed state of mind that had brought her close to a complete breakdown. She had been very ill and was still far from well.

The failure of her marriage had been a bad blow although she had contributed to it with her many flirtations. Working too hard, eating and sleeping badly, taking too many pills and drinking too much and living on her nerves had led to the inevitable. After some weeks of concentrated study and rehearsal and living it up at parties and nightclubs, Celeste had collapsed on stage on the first night of a much-publicised new play.

Rushed to a private clinic, she had been treated for nervous exhaustion and kept under sedation. When she eventually left the clinic for her Hampstead home, she was advised to rest and take proper care of herself and do no work for at least six months.

Attacked by a variety of morbid fears, feeling herself very much alone without the support of the husband she was in the process of divorcing or the friends she had alienated with her temperamental outbursts over the months, she had turned to Olivia. As children, they had been very close, but their lives had followed very different paths. There was an enormous gulf between a very successful actress and a hospital nurse.

Olivia was warm-hearted and sympathetic but very firm, all the qualities of a good nurse, and it suited her particularly well to fall in with the suggestion that she should spend the summer months looking after her cousin. Having just ended a six-month contract as a staff nurse at St Christopher's *and* her engagement to a houseman she had known since the early days of her training, she had seen all the advantages of playing the role of nurse cum companion to her beautiful and very famous cousin in the Riviera sunshine.

She was not exactly broken-hearted about Keith, but there was a dull ache of regret for the might-have-been in the region of her heart and a change of scene and circumstances might be a very good cure for it. Loving him had been more habit than truth, perhaps. But losing him had left a void in her life. She had been very fond of Keith and used to having him around and it had hurt to realise that the new theatre sister had become more important to him than herself. In the circumstances, what could a self-respecting girl do but hand back her ring and say that she had changed her mind about marrying him? Dear Keith. He had tried so hard to be regretful, but the relief had insisted on showing through. It was proof of his niceness that he had thoughtfully waited until she left Kit's before asking Mary Barnard to marry him.

She had been very happy during those years at Kit's, but she didn't think that she could ever go back. Not now. There came a time when one had to move on. New people, new places, new dreams for old . . .

There was certainly a world of difference between a busy surgical ward with its thirty patients in varying degree of pre- and post-operative condition and looking after one neurotic young woman. It was more a matter of psychological nursing than medical or surgical care . . . common-sense and firm handling, for the most part. She felt more like a nanny than a nurse at times, Olivia thought dryly—and at times she was very tempted to give her tiresome charge a good slap. But she was no more immune to Celeste's endearing charm than anyone else and she constantly made allowances for the girl who had been spoiled by too much too soon.

Poor little rich girl, Olivia sometimes called her with affectionate indulgence, but that didn't mean that she didn't sympathise and understand and want to help in every way she could. Celeste had been badly bruised—both mentally and emotionally—and it served no good purpose to declare that she had brought most of it on herself. She needed love and patient understanding and warm concern, not censure.

Child of a broken marriage, married much too young to a selfish and ambitious man, Celeste might have achieved fame and fortune in her theatrical career, but she had lost out on all the really important things in life. Or so it seemed to her thoughtful and caring cousin.

Thoughts wandering in very unprofessional fashion while doctor and patient discussed the many and various strains and stresses that had eventually taken their toll, Olivia was wrenched back to the present by the mention of her own name.

'. . . Olivia is a trained nurse, of course,' Celeste was explaining. 'She's very strict and makes me take all the right medicines at all the right times. Don't you, Livvy?'

Olivia smiled in polite acknowledgement of the humorous words as he turned to look at her. She abruptly realised that he was appraising her as a woman rather than as a nurse. She bridled instinctively at the too-male interest of an obviously sensual man. Her tiny waist and small tilting breasts, the slender hips and shapely legs, had known their fair share of admiration from amorous male patients and optimistic young doctors in the past. Somehow she had never resented those admiring and hopeful glances as much as she suddenly resented the way in which this doctor ran his gaze over her slight but perfectly-proportioned body.

He knew it, too. She saw the sudden gleam of amusement in the depths of his eyes. But his tone was formally and coolly professional as he reached for a phial of tablets from the tray that Olivia had prepared for his inspection and said: 'I should like Mrs Knight to stop taking these. I'll write up a prescription for something just as effective but not as habit-forming.'

'*I must sleep!*' Celeste exclaimed with the beginnings of panic in her lovely voice. 'I *need* my sleeping pills. Those are marvellous!'

He smiled, warmly reassuring. 'I'll give you some that are just as marvellous, Mrs Knight. In a very short time, I hope that you'll be sleeping well without the aid of any drugs. Sea air, exercise and a tranquil mind can work wonders, you know.' He rose with slight reluctance. 'I should like to stay and talk but I mustn't neglect my other patients. I'm one of your most fervent admirers, Mrs Knight. I saw your Ophelia at the National Theatre a few years ago.'

Celeste lay back on the cushions of the sofa and smiled at him, rather wanly. 'You must come to dinner one evening when I'm feeling less tired.'

'I should like that very much,' he said, very promptly.

There was a flattering warmth in the dark eyes. Being all woman, Celeste couldn't fail to notice it or to quicken slightly. Olivia hoped that her cousin wouldn't develop one of her tumultuous and short-lived passions for the man. They had quite enough on their plate without that kind of emotional turbulence to complicate matters!

She observed that he held Celeste's hand just a fraction longer than necessary as he took leave of his patient, assuring her that he would see her about the same time the next day. He managed to convey that it would be the bright spot of his busy day, Olivia thought dryly. A very practised charmer!

She accompanied him out to the hall and listened attentively to his precise instructions, the well-trained nurse with nothing in mind but the care and welfare of her patient.

'Light meals to tempt an obviously capricious appetite and no alcohol during the day. No more than two drinks each evening, enough to relax without stimulating. Early to bed after a warm bath and some soothing massage. I want her to take a walk along the beach every morning and afternoon. Encourage her to swim a little each day. No shopping trips, no parties and no other excitements until I say the word. Mrs Knight won't like the regime, I imagine. But she should certainly benefit from it.'

'Yes, Doctor.' Olivia thought dryly that Celeste would dislike it intensely and be very bored and everyone else would suffer for it.

'Don't thwart her unnecessarily but don't allow her to do exactly as she pleases, either,' he warned. He must have seen something in her expression for he smiled suddenly, taking her unawares with the warmth and charm of that understanding smile. 'She may not be very easy to handle for a few weeks but you look very capable, Nurse. Where did you train, by the way?' She saw his glance veer to the badge on her breast and thought that he stiffened slightly. 'Oh, yes . . . St Christopher's. Excellent!'

'The best,' she said lightly and with pride.

He smiled politely. 'Quite famous for its pretty nurses, too. Justified, I would say!'

Olivia was unimpressed by the hint of flattery in the words. She suspected that it was automatic and part of his stock in trade as a charmer. For no reason at all, a vague memory stirred and she said on a sudden, very unprofessional impulse: 'I believe I know you!'

'I don't think so.' He still smiled but there was a slightly guarded look in the dark eyes.

'Weren't you at Kit's a few years ago?'

'Before your time, I imagine,' he returned lightly. It was an admission that he was no stranger to the well-known hospital and a denial that she could possibly have known him or anything about him.

'Not quite,' she said slowly. She knew that she was being persistent and no doubt he thought her rude as well as pushing. But it was curious that he was being evasive when she knew instinctively that he had some past connection with Kit's. She looked up at him, quite unaware of the challenge in her grey and very direct eyes. 'Weren't you a registrar? Didn't people call you the Beau?'

He was obviously annoyed. Olivia saw the dull flush of anger creep into the handsome face beneath the warm tan. His eyes narrowed and he said coldly: 'If you remember that, then I daresay you recall the rest.'

There was *something*. An elusive memory. Some gossip about him and a staff nurse. She fancied he had left Kit's under a cloud. Perhaps that was why the unusual name had stuck in her mind, forgotten until she linked it with the man himself when she saw him.

Morgan Beauclerc. They had called him Beau not only as an obvious shortening of his surname but also because he had a reputation as a rake. He had been a very successful womaniser among all the pretty and impressionable junior nurses who had been so ready to fall into the arms of a very attractive and exciting man.

Having met Keith on almost her first day at Kit's, Olivia had taken very little notice of the good-looking registrar or the gossip about him. Their paths had never crossed and he had left Kit's soon after she began her training. Dark men were not much to her taste, anyway. She liked men who were blond and blue-eyed, rugged outdoor types. Morgan Beauclerc too obviously preferred indoor sports, she thought dryly.

She shook her head. 'I remember your name, that's all. We never met.'

He visibly relaxed. 'No,' he agreed, warmth returning to his smile. 'I wouldn't have forgotten you if we had.'

Olivia didn't respond to that blatant flattery. 'Is there anything else, Doctor?' She took refuge in formality, the etiquette between doctor and nurse that had been drilled into her so relentlessly during her training.

He took the hint, moved towards the door. 'I'll see that Mrs Knight has the new sleeping pills by tonight, Nurse. I've prescribed a tonic for her, too. But she will benefit most by following my advice—and I shall rely on you to see that she does!'

She closed the door and went back to Celeste, wondering what there was about Morgan Beauclerc that set all her instincts at danger. She knew that she distrusted him. But she wasn't sure if she was apprehensive for herself or for her too-vulnerable cousin!

'What on earth have you been talking about for so long?' Celeste was slightly petulant. She loved to be discussed but only in her hearing and only if she could be sure that everyone was saying nice things about her.

'Medical matters,' Olivia said briskly. 'We are going to put you right between us and you must be good and do just as you're told. He has some very sensible ideas, I think. I doubt if you'll agree with them.'

Celeste wrinkled her very pretty nose. 'Lucy said he was a marvellous doctor and would know just what to do for me. I hope she's right. What kind of ideas, Livvy?'

'You are to lead a very quiet life, for one thing. No visitors, no outings, no lengthy phone calls to friends or your agent. Plenty of rest, a sensible diet and some healthy exercise. I'm sure you'll feel very much better for it all.'

'I shall die of boredom,' Celeste announced gloomily.

'You aren't going to die of anything,' Olivia said firmly to deflect her cousin's morbid fears and fancies, so often aired with a kind of perverted pleasure in the thought that everyone would be sorry if she suffered a fatal heart attack or died from an incurable disease. 'Not until you're a very old lady and a dame of the British theatre. Shall we have some tea?'

'I'd rather have a drink. Get me a Martini, will you, Livvy?'

'I'm sorry. Drinks are out during the day and no more than two at night. Doctor's orders.'

'But that's ridiculous!' Celeste exclaimed angrily. 'I need a drink right now.'

'Darling, you're paying the man to give you advice,' Olivia said gently. 'If you ignore it, he won't give a damn. He'll just suggest that you should consult another doctor. Why don't you try his way before condemning it?'

'Two drinks a day and no more? Is that what he says? Very well! I'll have a Martini now and only one this evening!' Celeste declared gleefully, as delighted as a child with the sudden change of mood that was symptomatic of her illness. 'Make it a double, Livvy!'

Remembering that Morgan Beauclerc had told her not to thwart Celeste unnecessarily and knowing that her cousin could be coaxed into compromise but never forced into anything, Olivia laughed and crossed the room to the decanters. 'I'll keep you to that tonight,' she warned.

Celeste nestled deeper into the cushions of the long sofa, suddenly very tired. The brief stimulus of the doctor's visit had died away, leaving her drained. She seemed to have no energy for anything and very little interest in the days, each one as long and lonely as the last. On that thought, tears sprang to glisten in the beautiful eyes.

She was a lovely girl with ash-blonde hair shimmering on her shoulders and enormous eyes of so deep a blue that they seemed violet and the almost translucent skin of the true blonde. Tall and very slender with a superb figure and a natural grace, she was eye-catching. Her golden smile and a great deal of charm combined with undeniable acting ability had brought her fame and universal acclaim and a great deal of money before she was eighteen. Now, at twenty-four, she was ill and unhappy and convinced that her career had ended with her collapse. For what management would offer future contracts to an actress who had proved to be unreliable in health and temperament? Six months out of the public eye meant that she would be forgotten, finished!

Olivia set the glass on the table close to her cousin's hand. Then she drew up a low stool, sat down. 'What is it?' she asked gently.

The tears spilled, trickled down the pale cheeks. 'I hate this place. I want to go home,' Celeste said unreasonably. Only that morning, arriving at the Villa Paradis, she had been enchanted by its design, its lovely furnishings, its setting on the golden beach that was lapped by the warm waters of the Mediterranean. It had been the loveliest place in the world, just what she needed! Who could help feeling well and alive again very quickly in such surroundings? Now, her mood had changed to repudiate everything about it. 'This just isn't my scene, Livvy! I need people . . . not sand and sea and sun, for heaven's sake! I might as well be buried alive!' Abruptly, she covered her face with both hands.

Olivia leaned forward to stroke the soft fall of pale hair. She was fond of her cousin and her tender heart ached for Celeste who would probably be unhappy in any place that did not contain her husband. She had quarrelled with Tom countless times, flaunted other men and deliberately flouted his wishes, but it had all been done in the name of pride, Olivia suspected. Feeling herself unloved, there was no way that Celeste meant to admit to loving. Olivia was sure that all the symptoms of her cousin's illness sprang from loving and needing a man who had left her for another woman.

'Then we'll go home,' she soothed. 'In a few days when you've got over the effort of getting here.' She didn't tell her not to cry. Wisely, she knew that Celeste needed the outlet of those tears.

She went from the room and returned with some

warm water and a towel, some eau de cologne, a brush and comb.

Celeste submitted meekly to the freshening-up process and was then persuaded to adjourn to the terrace and relax in the shade of the palm trees that edged the villa. Olivia felt that the peaceful surroundings and the soothing murmur of the sea might act as a balm for the turmoil of mind and heart.

If she had been consulted instead of an English doctor with a French-sounding name and too much charm for his own or anyone else's good, Olivia would have recommended a very similar convalescence for Celeste. She felt that the frenetic pace of her cousin's life with its many conflicting demands of the past few years had not been conducive to health or sanity—and the shock of losing Tom must have been the last straw for a highly-strung and inevitably temperamental young woman.

Olivia knew something of heartache and humiliation for herself. Losing Keith hadn't been the end of her world, fortunately. But it had still hurt and she still missed the support of his affection and concern and interest. It took time and a sense of proportion to adjust one's thinking and feeling and living to a future that no longer seemed to hold the promise of happiness. She had always been a level-headed girl with sufficient strength of mind to cope with disappointments and disasters. By way of contrast, Celeste had always seemed so fragile and helpless, needing loving care and constant kindness to survive the 'slings and arrows of outrageous fortune'.

Olivia had known only a glimpse of the kind of hell that Celeste had suffered for months, but it had provided her with an insight that was invaluable at the present time. If only because Celeste knew of the broken engagement and its cause and felt that she understood and sympathised with her state of mind and heart where others did not.

Olivia leaned against the low stone wall that was the boundary between villa and beach and soaked in the warm sunshine and the lilting rhythm of the waves against the shore. She was prepared to feel that the lovely, tranquil surroundings would compensate in some measure for leaving Kit's and the kind of nursing she loved and her many friends. And in this idyllic spot, it might be possible for Celeste to relax and find pleasure in a simple, uncluttered way of life and to feel that she could make a new beginning, after all . . .

'Must you wear that awful outfit?' Celeste complained, tossing aside a magazine that had bored her within moments of picking it up, looking around for something to criticise. 'The colour just doesn't do anything for you, Livvy. I know you brought some pretty frocks. Do go and change into one of them!'

Olivia turned, smiling. 'Now you know it's my Kit's uniform, Celeste—and I told you that I was putting it on to impress Dr Beauclerc,' she said lightly.

'And was he impressed?'

It was too quick, slightly suspicious. Olivia laughed reassuringly. 'Darling, he didn't even notice me! He was much too busy admiring you!' She was thankful that it was the truth. Celeste was in no mood to tolerate male attentions being centred on anyone but herself. Heaven knew she needed the boost to her ego and morale! Olivia had not the least need or the slightest desire to attract the man's interest.

Celeste smiled, spirits lifting slightly. Flirtation was second nature to her even though she was still very much in love with her husband. She had never been able to resist the charm of an attractive man. And Dr Morgan Beauclerc was just as charming and just as attractive as Lucy Bellamy had declared.

That might be the only redeeming feature about her unwilling sojourn in an isolated villa on the Mediterranean coast . . .

CHAPTER TWO

WHETHER by chance or design, Dr Beauclerc called again just as they had finished dinner that evening.

'Don't let me disturb you,' he said briskly on the heels of the announcement of his name. 'I had to visit a patient just along the avenue and thought I'd deliver the tablets and tonic that I prescribed for you, Mrs Knight.'

Celeste began to sparkle and a little colour flew into her lovely face. Tired and listless, she had scarcely eaten anything although the Bellamys employed a superb cook. She had sat in moody silence throughout the meal, refusing to respond to any of Olivia's conversational ventures.

Suddenly, with the arrival of a man, and a very attractive one at that, she came alive. 'How very kind! Please—do come and join me in my solitary Martini! You see that I am being very good and obeying doctor's orders!'

She was looking very lovely in floating, flame-coloured chiffon. She had insisted that they should dress for dinner. Standards must be maintained, she had declared. One must always be prepared for the unexpected. Now, she threw a triumphant glance at Olivia in her simple dinner frock of dull-gold jersey silk.

Moving into the room at that warm invitation, Morgan Beauclerc also glanced at Olivia. Meeting the dark and slightly curious eyes, she smiled coolly. 'Good evening, Doctor. Shall I take charge of those?' She held out her hand for the package. Their hands brushed briefly in the exchange. Not even by the flicker of an eyelid did she betray the odd and quite unexpected reaction of her flesh to the physical contact with a man she was not at all sure that she liked and was quite sure that she had good reason to distrust—if only she could remember what it was!

She did not trust Celeste, either. So she hurried from the room to lock away the sleeping pills with the other drugs prescribed for her cousin and which could be dangerous in the wrong hands. She did not think that Celeste would ever mean to take her own life. She did think that her impulsive and very volatile cousin might make a bid for attention and sympathy and the return of a repentant husband with an attempted overdose if opportunity and mood ever coincided. So she was not taking any chances and she kept the key of the small leather drugs case safely hidden in her room.

Before returning to doctor and patient, Olivia glanced at herself in the long mirror and decided that the clinging silk flattered her slender figure. The warm colouring of her favourite frock brought out the gold glints in her chestnut curls and complemented the creamy warmth of her skin. She was a pretty girl but few people noticed when she was in the company of her beautiful cousin. Celeste's exquisite loveliness overshadowed most women, in fact.

She was standing close to Morgan Beauclerc when Olivia went into the room, the lovely face tilted up to him, her hand resting on his arm in unspoken and quite unmistakable invitation. He was smiling and the look in his dark eyes was equally unmistakable, Olivia thought on a sudden surge of irritation. He had advised against any kind of excitement for his patient and yet he was evoking the worst possible kind with the admiration and the ardour in his gaze.

It seemed very obvious that he had made an excuse to call at the Villa Paradis that evening just to see Celeste again—and her cousin was delighted!

'Mrs Knight was just about to retire to her room,' she said firmly, far from caring if the words were too pointed with implication. 'It's been a very long and tiring day.'

'Why are we so formal?' Celeste demanded impatiently. 'Must I be *Mrs Knight*? It can't be necessary! I shall certainly call you *Morgan* rather than *Dr Beauclerc*,' she declared, smiling at him warmly. 'I know that you and I are going to be great friends. I always do know about people, don't I, Livvy?'

She was a terrible judge of character, in fact. But Olivia didn't say so. 'It's a matter of medical etiquette,' she said lightly, reminding him as much as Celeste. 'Doctors aren't supposed to be too friendly with their patients.' Women patients, she amended silently. There didn't seem to be any bar to friendship between a doctor and a male patient. They were often members of the same clubs, entertaining each other and attending the same parties.

'How absurd!' Celeste exclaimed crossly, sinking into the cushions of the sofa with an air of petulance.

Morgan Beauclerc smiled. 'I do agree, Mrs Knight. It is absurd in some cases. But I'd rather not run the risk of being reported to the British Medical Association for unprofessional conduct by your dragon of a nurse!'

The warm laughter in eyes and voice tried to embrace Olivia but she refused to be amused or charmed. She continued to move about the room, gathering up her cousin's scattered and varied possessions in readiness for ushering her firmly off to bath and bed. She found herself wishing wryly that she did not have to play the part of nanny to a very spoiled and wilful child.

Celeste abruptly decided to take offence with her usual unpredictability of mood. 'Very well,' she declared coldly, chin tilting and eyes flashing. 'I'm sure there are plenty of doctors in Nice or Antibes who will be delighted to take care of me and won't snub a friendly overture!'

His smile deepened. 'Certainly. But not one of them is as clever or as amusing, you'll find,' he drawled, eyes dancing.

Celeste looked at him quickly, eyes narrowed. Then she laughed. 'Or as conceited!' she capped lightly, flirtatiously. Her eyes began to sparkle. 'Lucy Bellamy says you are dangerous, too. Was she one of your patients?' she challenged.

'No. One of my flirts,' he told her outrageously, a twinkle in the dark eyes. 'As a result, she recommends me to all her friends!'

Recognising the danger signals in those too bright eyes and flushed cheeks and the very brittle laugh, Olivia thought it time to intervene. 'We are keeping the doctor from his dinner,' she said firmly, knowing that she sounded like the dragon of a nurse that he had declared. 'It's time for your bath, too. Shall I tell Yvonne to run it for you?'

Abruptly brought down to earth from the dangerous heights, Celeste sobered. 'I'll tell her myself,' she decided. She held out her hand to the tall and very attractive man. 'Will you come to see me tomorrow? I don't mean everything I say, you know.'

Morgan took the slight hand in both his own and looked down at the enchantingly troubled face with warm understanding. 'When you are well enough not to need me as a doctor, I shall be delighted to be your friend, Mrs Knight,' he said gently.

'Then I must hurry and get well . . .' With tears obviously threatening, Celeste tugged her hand from his clasp and ran from the room.

He looked after her, the smile lingering about the sensual mouth and more than a touch of sympathy blending with the admiration in those dark eyes, Olivia thought. She said quietly: 'I don't know if you are a shocking flirt or a clever psychologist.'

He turned quickly, laughed. 'Both, of course!'

Olivia glanced away from the mischievous devil in the dancing eyes, suddenly convinced that he was too attractive for any woman's peace of mind—and knew it too well!

'Do you encourage all your women patients to fall in love with you?' she asked, more curious than critical.

A flicker of surprise crossed the handsome face at her perception. 'Only the beautiful ones,' he returned, amused by the direct and challenging question.

'It's unethical.' She forced tartness into her tone.

'It can also be therapeutic in certain cases.' He was suddenly serious, the doctor discussing a patient with the attendant nurse. 'She's a very disturbed young woman. To coin a phrase, she's a storm-tossed ship badly in need of a reliable anchor.'

Olivia resisted the impulse to ask if he saw himself as either reliable or a rock of strength where the lovely and rather lovable Celeste was concerned.

'She needs her husband,' she said bluntly, not mincing matters. Romantic phrases were all very well. A practical approach to his patient's needs would serve her better!

He raised an eyebrow. 'There's a degree of sexual frustration, no doubt. I might prescribe the remedy. I won't be so unprofessional as to provide it, I promise you,' he said, very dry, aware of her dislike and disapproval and distrust and knowing the reason for it. It was damnably annoying that she should be a Kit's nurse and must have heard all the scurrilous gossip that had attached to his name some years ago.

Olivia shrugged off the reassurance with the contempt it deserved. 'I suppose that comes into it. I'm not sure that it's as important to a woman as men always imagine,' she said briskly, unconsciously betraying her own state of virginity to a man who knew a great deal about women and could not help being rather intrigued by this one.

'Men might imagine. Doctors have hard facts to work on,' he reminded her, his tone warning her to keep personalities out of the discussion.

Olivia felt rebuked. A little colour rushed into her face. 'I was really referring to the fact that Mrs Knight is very unhappy about the pending divorce,' she said firmly. 'She's very much in love with her husband and doesn't want to lose him and doesn't know how to hold him. She was shattered when he didn't rush to her side when she was so ill. But that's the kind of man he is, I'm afraid. Although I wouldn't waste my breath trying to convince her that he isn't worth the way she feels about him!'

Morgan studied her thoughtfully, interested in the

passionate concern of this serious young nurse for a patient from a very different world. 'You are obviously something of a psychologist, too,' he said, with quiet approval. 'Do you feel that her breakdown was psychosomatic?'

'To some extent. Helped by the life she's been leading for too long. But that isn't psychology, Doctor. That's just knowing her well and caring enough to want her to be happy.'

He smiled, slightly puzzled. 'Perhaps. But how do you come to know her so well, Nurse Paine? I understood that you had only been with her for a few weeks.' His curiosity had finally got the better of him.

'We're cousins. We grew up together,' Olivia said simply.

Now that he knew of the relationship, he detected a trace of family likeness in that oval face. But she was merely pretty whereas Celeste Knight was one of the loveliest women he had ever known, quite breath-taking with that pale and delicate beauty that stirred an instinctive chivalry in a man's breast.

Better known to audiences as Celeste Carr, he remembered her vividly as Ophelia and the memory of her exquisite loveliness had never been erased. Morgan wondered wryly if he had been a little in love with her ever since. She was certainly an enchanting creature and even lovelier with that air of frailty and utter helplessness.

He nodded. 'I see. That explains a great deal, you know. She's obviously fond of you and also dependent on you to some extent. You're more than a friend and very much more than a professional nurse. You're family. Someone she can trust, someone to turn to when others fail—and that's very important in her present state of mind. She needs you.'

'I expect we need each other,' Olivia said, matter of fact. 'She's all the family I have these days.' Suddenly fearful that she might have sounded emotional, convincing him that he was dealing with a couple of neurotics, she added briskly: 'I must attend to my patient! She's probably forgotten all about her bath. She's very easily distracted at the moment. Just like a child.'

'And I must get back to my long-delayed dinner.' Morgan smiled, suddenly warm. 'I'm glad I decided to call in this evening. You've clarified one or two points that were puzzling me.'

'Clarify one for me,' Olivia returned lightly, accompanying him to the door. 'How *did* you get your unusual name, Dr Beauclerc?'

He laughed. 'It isn't much of a puzzle. My father was French. My mother is Welsh.'

It was a dangerous mixture, Olivia thought swiftly. The hot blood of the Gauls and the vein of romantic sensitivity of the Celts. No wonder he was so attractive to women. He was probably one of that very rare breed, a rake with a tendency to fall lightly in love with the women he pursued. Most rakes were entirely without heart or conscience and very little threat to a woman's peace of mind. Morgan Beauclerc might not be so easily dismissed . . .

Her anxiety was all for Celeste. Suppose her cousin fell out of love with Tom and into love with a man who might be just as unreliable, hurt her just as badly. She didn't think Celeste could take another blow of that nature. She could only hope that Morgan Beauclerc knew just what he was doing when he toyed with the delicate balance of Celeste's emotional and mental stability.

He drove away and Olivia went in search of her cousin. She found her on the terrace, defiantly pouring herself a drink from the trolley. Olivia knew immediately that it was not the first that Celeste had enjoyed behind her back.

She paused on the threshold, knowing that only fools rushed in. Olivia had never been a fool. She studied her lovely cousin. A little breeze from the sea was toying with the floating panels of her long dress, stirring the fine blonde hair on her shoulders. The light fell full on her face, wet with tears.

Olivia moved forward. 'How many have you had?' she asked gently.

Celeste shrugged. 'No idea.'

'Try to remember. I can't give you a sleeping pill on top of alcohol, you know.'

Celeste turned swiftly. 'Nonsense!'

'It isn't nonsense. It's extremely dangerous,' she said firmly.

Celeste hesitated. 'Only one.'

Olivia didn't believe her. She sighed. 'Why?'

'Why not?' She was cold, regarding Olivia with dislike. 'Has he gone? You spent enough time taking me to pieces and putting me together again, didn't you? Why the hell did you tell him about Tom?'

'A doctor can't give you the right treatment unless he knows all about you,' Olivia said lightly. There was no point in being cross with her for listening. She ought to have remembered that the open windows led out to the terrace and, knowing Celeste, should have been instantly suspicious of her readiness to leave them alone together.

'I'm *not* in love with Tom. Why won't you listen when I tell you! It was kid stuff. I grew out of it in six months. I don't want him back—ever! That bitch he's with is welcome to him. I mean it, Olivia. And I'll thank you not to queer my pitch with every man who fancies me by telling him that I love my husband!'

Her voice had risen steadily throughout the tirade. Suddenly she smashed the delicate glass in her hand to the ground and burst into uncontrollable sobs that shook her slender frame.

Olivia held her and soothed her like a child and gradually quietened her enough to persuade her to lie down on her bed while her bath was prepared.

She left her only briefly. When she went back, Celeste was deeply asleep, her cheek cradled on her hand. Olivia looked down at her, moved by the enchantment and deceptive innocence of that lovely face. She looked so young, so untouched by the anguish of recent months. She was an exquisite flower with a disease lurking within the delicate petals, she thought sadly. It was not surprising that Morgan Beauclerc had responded so instinctively to that femininity and fragility. He might be a doctor but he was also a man like any other.

Rather than disturb Celeste, Olivia brought a light cover and laid it gently over the slight figure. The lovely dress would crumple but that was unimportant. Celeste was sleeping without the aid of pills for the first time in weeks. Perhaps it was too many Martinis. Perhaps it was the effect of too much emotion. And perhaps it was the undeniable comfort for a lost and lonely woman of knowing that she had attracted the admiration and interest of a very personable man.

Able to relax for the first time that day, Olivia suddenly discovered that she was tired, too. It was a warm night and the house seemed airless despite the open windows. Not daring to go too far in case Celeste should wake and want her, she walked down the beach to the edge of the sea.

The moon shimmered on the surface of the water and the night was very still. Olivia knew a strange, haunting melancholy of mood as she looked out to the dark-edged horizon. For no reason at all, she found herself thinking of Morgan Beauclerc and discovered that his attractive face was etched very vividly on her mind's eye.

She wished she could remember what she had once known about him. But it was nearly five years ago and she had not really listened at the time to a scandal concerning people she did not know. Whatever he had done, it could not have been so very bad, even if he had left Kit's in a hurry, for his name was still on the medical register. But it must have been bad enough to bring him across the Channel to a private practice in France.

But he was French, of course, she remembered suddenly. Perhaps it had always been his intention to return to his native land once he had his doctorate. It was clever of him to choose to practise in an area that was choc-a-bloc with wealthy and frequently titled English society, types who sometimes had little of interest in their lives but needless concern for their health. He had good looks, a great deal of charm and a fluent command of their language as well as a clever grasp of psychology and she didn't doubt that he was very popular in such circles.

Thinking of a virtual stranger unaccountably turned her thoughts to Keith. Olivia waited for the slight contraction of her heart for all that they had meant to each other and all that she had lost when he fell out of love. With a slight shock of surprise, she discovered that it no longer hurt to think of Keith and the might-have-been.

She only felt a rush of warm tenderness for the memory of him and past happiness. They had been good days, happy days, memories to treasure as a souvenir of youthful and untarnished optimism for the future. Keith had been a very valuable part of her growing-up years and she was glad to have known and loved him.

Perhaps one day she would love again, a love enriched by the knowledge of how it ought to be between mature man and woman. She might not care to recall how she had tingled at the fleeting touch of Morgan Beauclerc's hand or how his sudden smile had sparked an odd quiver of excitement in the secret places of her body. But she had become aware all in a moment that there had been a very important lack in her relationship with Keith. Loving him, she had never quickened with sexual desire or longed to know the power and glory of passion in his arms. To protect him from hurt, she had pretended a response to his ardour. She had pretended to be old-fashioned enough to want to remain a virgin until they married, too. If he suspected her frigidity, he had never accused her of it. But it might have been one of the reasons why he had fallen out of love with her, she thought perceptively.

Sometimes she had felt anxious about her lack of physical response to his tentative lovemaking, but comforted herself with the thought that it was a mental block due to her upbringing and that she would be as passionate and responsive as any husband could wish once she wore a wedding ring.

Now, Olivia wondered if the chemistry had been all wrong. For her body had responded readily enough to the very dangerous attraction of a man she scarcely knew. Morgan Beauclerc was much too exciting for her peace of mind, she thought wryly. Fortunately, he was not at all interested in her or her virginity might be at risk. For she had suddenly realised the potency of his sexuality, his animal magnetism, his very physical brand of charm. For the first time, she became aware that a woman's virginity depended not so much on caution but on the degree of temptation!

And Morgan Beauclerc was a great deal of temptation for any woman . . .

'*C'est une belle nuit, Mademoiselle . . .*'

Olivia spun at the soft words, relaxed as she recognised the fair hair and stocky build of their near neighbour, seen earlier in the day as he strode across the beach and waved a friendly hand to them as they sat on the terrace.

'*Oui, tres belle*,' she agreed, friendly but preparing to walk back to the house. The beach was deserted and she did not mean to be unduly encouraging to an unknown Frenchman. Young, curly-haired with an engaging smile, he wore the universal jeans and sweatshirt and looked like a student. She had a sudden vision of him playing guitar—and playing it well.

He fell into step beside her. 'Jean-Paul Dornier. We are neighbours,' he said, slipping smoothly into English as he introduced himself, smiling.

'Yes, I know.' Olivia tried not to quicken her steps, not wishing to offend with a seeming suspicion of an approach that was probably no more than friendly interest in newcomers.

'You prefer that we speak English? May I know your name?'

'Olivia Paine. I'm not very fluent in your language, I'm afraid. I can only manage schoolgirl French.'

He shrugged in Gallic fashion. 'No matter. I speak very good English,' he assured her without conceit. 'Lucy has telephoned me. I am delighted to be of any possible assistance to you and your friend.'

'Cousin,' she corrected. 'Celeste is my cousin. You are very kind, M. Dornier. Thank you.' It was easier to be polite than to turn down his offer, she decided. He seemed a pleasant and harmless young man.

'Please! *Jean-Paul!*'

It was impossible to resist the warm and eager friendliness of his smile. Any more than she could have kicked away a puppy bounding about her feet! She had reached the gate in the wall and she opened it, smiled at him. 'My cousin may be needing me,' she said lightly so that he wouldn't feel rebuffed. 'She hasn't been well and is convalescing.'

'Lucy tells me everything,' he said, nodding. 'You are a nurse, *n'est ce pas*? I shall come to you with fevered brow.' His eyes danced with mischief.

'I shall be much too busy to notice,' Olivia said, laughing.

'You will notice me,' he said confidently. 'I shall be of much use. You do not drive, I think? I shall be pleased to take you anywhere you wish. I am an excellent driver and my car is reliable. I am also the perfect dinner guest. I do not drink too much and I talk a lot—and I invite myself because I cannot resist Marthe's cooking!' He held out his hand, smiling. 'Tomorrow?'

Olivia gave him her hand and was amused when he

lifted it to his lips and kissed it with a Gallic flourish.

'About seven? We dine early,' she told him in tacit agreement. He had an infectious gaiety that would probably be very good for Celeste who did indeed need people just as she had said. Her spirits would probably lift at the discovery that this personable young man wished to be their friend. Olivia liked him. So would Celeste.

'Excellent! I shall amuse your cousin and make light love to you—*oui*?'

'*Non*!' she said, very firmly.

But her eyes smiled if her lips did not and he turned away, chuckling . . .

CHAPTER THREE

OLIVIA told Celeste about her brief encounter with the young Frenchman at breakfast. She didn't think that her cousin was really listening but it didn't matter. Celeste brightened visibly at the mention of a dinner guest.

Then she slumped. 'I'm not supposed to be enjoying myself. Doctor's orders!'

Olivia smiled. 'It's possible that Dr Beauclerc knows Jean-Paul. I'll ask if he objects when he calls this morning. If he does, I'll explain that you aren't well enough yet for even an informal dinner-party. I'm sure Jean-Paul will understand.'

Celeste looked at her suspiciously. 'Who is this Jean-Paul? You seem to know a lot about him for a brief encounter on the beach! What were you doing on the beach at midnight, anyway?'

'It wasn't midnight,' Olivia protested, choosing to be amused rather than to resent her cousin's tone. 'I wanted a breath of sea air before going to bed. Jean-Paul Dornier. He lives just along the beach. He waved to us yesterday. Don't you remember? The boy in the orange shirt who took out the boat?'

'I don't remember *boys*!'

'Well, he isn't a boy, exactly,' Olivia amended hastily. 'Twenty-three or four, I suppose. Fair people always look so much younger.' She smiled at Celeste. '*You* look about seventeen in those shorts!'

It was perfectly true, but it had still been calculated to

chase away the ill-humour – and it worked. Celeste smiled with the complacent confidence of a woman who knows herself to be beautiful. The brief white shorts set off long, tanned legs and the flimsy shirt more than hinted at the curve of beautiful bare breasts thrusting against the thin material. Olivia thought dryly of the inevitable effect of all that beauty on a sensual man—and didn't doubt that Celeste was looking forward to the doctor's visit.

'Dornier, did you say? I think Lucy might have mentioned that name,' Celeste conceded with casual indifference. 'Like him, do you? Don't make a fool of yourself over another man, Livvy. I don't intend to—ever again!' She reached for the coffee-pot, refilled her cup.

'Darling, couldn't you eat a morsel of scrambled egg?' Olivia coaxed gently, ignoring the bitter words of advice. 'I know you aren't hungry, but Marthe went to so much trouble to tempt your appetite with this rather special recipe. She's a sweet old thing, isn't she? And so concerned about you. She thinks you are much too thin.'

'Compared with Marthe, everyone is much too thin.' Celeste was caustic about the Bellamys' massive but excellent cook-housekeeper who went with the villa. But she didn't protest when Olivia set the plate before her. She picked up a fork and toyed with the food and even ate one or two mouthfuls. Olivia carefully did not comment, getting on with her own breakfast.

Later, Celeste flatly refused to go for the recommended walk. 'It's too hot,' she said petulantly although there was a gentle, alleviating breeze that morning. 'I'm tired. I didn't sleep at all. Why didn't I have my pill, Livvy? What have you done with them, anyway? The wonder drug that Morgan claims are better than Nembutal! I couldn't find the tablets anywhere. You were sleeping like a log. Do you know that? You're supposed to look after me, Livvy. I might have died in the night!'

Petulance had turned to genuine apprehension and dismay. Olivia recognised that it was a very real fear for the sick girl although there was absolutely no basis for it. Organically, Celeste was as sound as a bell. Physically, after some weeks of complete rest, she was in excellent health.

Yet frequently, without apparent rhyme or reason to trigger it, she suffered all the classic symptoms of anxiety. The rapid pulse, the sweating, the uncontrollable trembling that shook her slight frame from head to toe, the panic-induced sense of suffocation that was followed by the inevitable faint. Every time, Celeste was sure that it had been a minor heart attack and no one would admit it. Every time, she was sure that the next one would bring about her death.

Test after test had shown that there was nothing wrong with her heart. Celeste would not be convinced. Everyone was conspiring to keep the truth from her, she declared. And if it wasn't her heart, then she was slowly dying from an incurable cancer and no one had the courage to tell her so! She could face up to the truth, she insisted. Not knowing was killing her!

She dreaded to sleep because she thought she might die—and so she could not sleep without the aid of drugs. She dreaded each new day with its lack of meaning, the constant weariness of body and soul, the flat feeling of depression and the minor disappointments that loomed so large in her suddenly empty days.

Celeste missed the glamour and excitement and the

adrenalin-boosting demands of her work, but she declared that she didn't want to walk into another theatre for as long as she lived or see another television studio.

She longed for the company of people and the stimulus of the show-business social whirl, but she insisted that everyone tired and bored her and she just wanted to be left alone.

She needed her friends desperately but lately she had been rude to them and quarrelled with them and done her best to alienate them, one after the other. Now, she felt that she had no one but Olivia. And she clung to her with both hands like a frightened and bewildered child. Loving her like a sister, Olivia ached for her unhappiness and despair and did what she could to help and comfort.

She didn't point out that twice she had left her bed in the night to check on her patient, satisfying herself that Celeste was sleeping and comfortable. She merely smiled and apologised meekly for her lack of consideration and settled Celeste on a lounger on the terrace with some magazines, a tray of iced drinks and the embroidery that she sewed so exquisitely when she was in the mood and might pick up for a few moments during the course of the morning . . . as long as it was never tactlessly suggested that it was much-needed occupational therapy, Olivia thought dryly.

She brought the telephone, at Celeste's insistence, and placed it on the low table. She knew that as soon as her back was turned, her cousin would call one of her few remaining friends and talk interminably about nothing in the hope of gleaning the smallest item of news about Tom Knight in the process of the conversation. It was not in Olivia's nature to hate anyone. But there were moments when she felt that she hated Tom Knight for what he had done to Celeste—and, most of all, for not caring!

She had liked Tom. Everyone did. And Celeste had fallen passionately, violently, tumultuously in love. He had married her within a month – and Olivia had never been able to understand *why*. Because he so obviously did not love her at all. She had hoped with all her heart that it would never be obvious to Celeste, too . . . and watched that first radiant happiness falter and fade with the passing months. Everyone but Celeste had known that the marriage was doomed—and no doubt she had known it in her heart and begun to build the defences that had crumbled so dramatically on that disastrous opening night.

She would not talk about that night. But Olivia had learned from other members of the cast that Tom had sat in the front row of the stalls with the woman he had been living with since he left Celeste. In the middle of the most critical scene of the entire play, he had suddenly got up from his seat and strode down the centre aisle and out of the theatre. It must have been the final humiliation for a tense and overwrought Celeste. Only moments later she had dried, completely forgetting her lines, and then collapsed in a crumpled heap.

It had made headlines in all the national newspapers. But Tom had ignored his wife's illness and refused to talk to the press.

Olivia wondered why Celeste didn't hate him, too . . .

Jean-Paul strolled across the beach with his arms full of flowers, their bright colours vying with his vivid, multi-coloured shirt and matching Bermuda shorts. He leaned on the low wall. '*Bonjour!*' he said, sure of a welcome.

Olivia smiled, liking the glowing good looks and the easy friendliness. She rose from her chair and went to speak to him. '*Bonjour! Comment ça va?*' Her tone was warmer than she knew.

His eyes twinkled, a little mischief in their blue depths. '*Très bien!* At least you *try*!'

She laughed at his teasing. 'My accent is terrible. At least I admit it!' she countered lightly.

'Your accent is non-existent,' he corrected gently. 'I shall fall in love with you, nonetheless.' His smile deepened as a little colour stole into her face.

Celeste tossed aside her magazine, abruptly deigning to notice him. 'Oh, it's you,' she said, indifferent.

Jean-Paul climbed over the low wall without invitation and approached her, holding out the mass of flowers. 'For Madame,' he said with a flourish and a very enchanting smile.

Surprised, she took them. 'They're lovely . . .'

'So is Madame.' He made her a little bow, very French.

'*M'sieu est galant . . .*' She allowed him a swift, golden smile.

'*Quel accent!*' he exclaimed in mock amazement, eyes dancing. '*Superbe!*' He flashed a mischievous glance at an amused Olivia. Then he turned back to Celeste. 'You may call me Jean-Paul!' he declared with the air of bestowing the supreme accolade.

Celeste laughed.

It was the most natural sound that Olivia had heard her cousin utter since her illness and she warmed even more to the likeable young Frenchman who had evoked it. She moved forward. 'I'll find vases and put your lovely flowers in water.'

She went away, leaving them together . . . and heard Celeste laugh again, soft and musical, as she entered the house.

Jean-Paul was going to be very good for Celeste, she suspected. He might even be good for her, too! He was young, he was fun. He reminded her of Keith with his well-brushed golden curls and blue eyes and fair skin, the warm smile and friendly manner.

She felt that he was a man to like, to trust, a man whose company she could enjoy because he wouldn't make any demands on her that she couldn't meet. He was no threat to an unsuspected and rather alarming sensuality or to her peace of mind, she thought thankfully . . .

And almost jumped out of her skin at the sound of Morgan Beauclerc's voice behind her as she arranged flowers in a vase in the spacious sitting-room. They had been expecting him, but she had been so absorbed in thinking about him while her hands were busy with the flowers that the ring at the bell hadn't registered and she hadn't realised that he had been admitted by Yvonne, the little maid who helped Marthe in the house.

Olivia turned, clutching a spray of flowers to her breast, annoyed with herself for that betraying start of surprise. 'Oh! Good morning, Doctor!'

She wasn't aware that she looked absurdly young and extremely pretty in the short summer frock in a fashionable shade of soft green that bared her arms and much of her slender legs, already sun-kissed to a slight and becoming tan. She had tied back her bright curls with a ribbon of the same shade to stop them tumbling about her face.

Morgan looked into the wide grey eyes with their thick fringe of long, dark lashes. The shining innocence in their depths shamed the flicker of desire that her slim figure and enchanting prettiness had evoked so unexpectedly.

He said lightly: 'You are not on duty this morning, Miss Paine?'

'But I am,' she assured him firmly. She put down the flowers. 'I'm wearing my badge.' She had pinned it to the bodice of her frock. 'My cousin doesn't like me to wear my uniform, you see. It reminds her that she has been ill.'

He nodded. 'How is she today?'

'Quite cheerful, at the moment.' Olivia explained about Jean-Paul, a little anxiously, recalling that he had stressed no visitors, no excitement. She mentioned the fact. 'I hope I didn't do wrong. But he isn't easy to snub,' she added.

'No, indeed,' he agreed with slight amusement, knowing Jean-Paul. 'But he's quite harmless. If Mrs Knight has taken a liking to him then there's no reason to snub him. I know you won't allow her to become overtired.'

'Then you won't object if he dines with us this evening?'

Morgan raised an eyebrow. 'I'm a doctor, not a dictator. I advise, that's all. If your cousin limits her drinks and goes to bed at a reasonable hour and the evening doesn't turn into a riot, she may entertain anyone she pleases.'

Olivia had never been in the habit of blindly obeying her impulses. But she heard herself saying, all in a rush:

'Perhaps you would join us, Doctor? Then I can be sure that she'll behave herself!'

He was about to refuse, to explain that he was dining with friends. But she turned such an unconsciously eager face to him that he didn't have the heart to do so.

'Thank you. I shall be delighted to combine a little work with a great deal of pleasure,' he said, eyes twinkling, consigning his friends to the limbo of another day without a qualm. A doctor could always plead pressure of work in such circumstances.

Olivia smiled, doubting that the compliment was meant for herself. He was too obviously interested in Celeste, not only as a patient but also as a possible conquest when she was no longer in need of his medical services.

She took him out to the terrace.

Celeste was animated, sparkling, extremely beautiful and she greeted him like an old friend, hands outstretched and her lovely smile offering a warm welcome.

'How are you?' he asked, clasping her hands and smiling down at her as she lay at full length on the lounger in the sun.

'I'm a fraud!' she declared gaily. 'I feel fine!'

'Excellent!' He placed strong fingers on the racing pulse in the slender wrist, observed the too-quick rise and fall of the beautiful breasts beneath the thin shirt. 'I wish all my patients responded so well to my treatment,' he said lightly. But he glanced at the attentive Olivia with a faint frown in the dark eyes.

Experienced in the reading of such messages, she crossed the terrace to speak to Jean-Paul. He had risen from his chair with a friendly nod for the doctor and then moved to stand by the low wall, courteously out of earshot. She touched his arm, spoke softly. He nodded. She walked with him to the low gate and watched him swing away across the beach with the beginnings of affection in her gaze. Then she returned to doctor and patient.

'. . . I should like to examine you thoroughly,' he was saying. 'Not here—and not today. At the Clinic, we have the most up-to-date equipment. I know you have had all the tests. But every doctor likes to satisfy himself that nothing has been overlooked.'

'Carry out any test you like,' Celeste said quickly. 'I should like to be satisfied of the same thing! But you must tell me if you find anything! I must know! No one will tell me the truth, you see—not even Livvy! I can't trust anyone!' She caught at his hand. 'But I'm sure I can trust *you*!' she declared warmly, smiling at him in the way that had encouraged too many men to fall in love.

Seeing the instant response in the dark eyes, Olivia doubted that he would prove to be an exception—and something stirred in her breast that might almost be jealousy. It was absurd, she knew. But he was a very attractive man and for the first time in her life she wished that she had been blessed with the kind of beauty that caught and held such a man's interest. She had never been envious of Celeste until that moment, she thought wryly.

'I'll show you the result of each test and make sure that you understand what it means,' he told Celeste, reassuring. 'Then you may really believe that you are a healthy young woman who has merely been overdoing things.'

Celeste visibly relaxed. 'Thank you! That's more than any other doctor has done for me!'

He glanced at Olivia, a surprised query in his eyes.

She shook her head slightly to convey that her cousin was in no mood to be fair to the many doctors who had already tried to help her—and saw the ready understanding that leaped to replace the startled expression.

He rose, tall and impressive, very debonair in the formal suit and so handsome that Olivia felt her pulses quicken without rhyme or reason.

'I mustn't stay,' he said with convincing regret. 'I have a long list of calls to make. But I shall look forward to seeing you this evening.'

Celeste smiled a query. 'Dr Beauclerc has agreed to join us for a very informal dinner,' Olivia said hastily, suddenly remembering that her cousin had not yet been told.

'Oh . . . ?' Celeste did not look at all pleased and Olivia's heart sank slightly. Then she realised that her cousin was annoyed that she had been forestalled. For she said, a little petulantly: 'How very nice! But I meant to ask you myself, you know.'

He smiled. 'I quite understand that the invitation came from you, Mrs Knight,' he said gently.

Olivia smiled at him gratefully, glad of his quick understanding and adroit handling of her difficult cousin.

'I wish you would call me Celeste!' she exclaimed, rueful. 'It makes it so difficult to think of you as a friend when you persist in being so formal!'

'I suspect that you delight in twisting your friends about your little finger,' he returned, eyes twinkling. 'I think it's safer that you should continue to think of me as your doctor. For the time being, anyway. You see, I intend to be very strict with you for a few weeks.'

'Oh, very well!' she agreed between amusement and

annoyance. 'But I refuse to call you anything but Morgan. It suits you!' She looked at him, head slightly to one side, abruptly deciding to come down on the side of laughter. 'Wasn't there a famous pirate of that name? You have the dashing and rather romantic look of a pirate, you know!' She smiled at him with admiration and a hint of coquetry in the beautiful blue eyes.

'My Welsh ancestry, perhaps,' he suggested, amused.

'Lucy told me that you're only half-French, I remember. You're in partnership with a brother, aren't you?'

'Half-brother,' he corrected. 'Gerard runs the clinic. You'll meet him when you come into town for the tests.' He glanced at his slim gold watch. 'I really must go . . . and you must rest, Mrs Knight. *Au 'voir!*'

He explained in some detail the various tests he had in mind. Olivia listened carefully, confirmed that all of them had been carried out in London without showing any abnormality.

'There isn't anything wrong at all,' she said firmly. 'Not physically, not now. She was very tired, very tense, emotionally strung-up—and we both know that the body has its own methods for forcing someone like Celeste to slow down and treat it with more respect.'

'Certainly. I don't think there is any medical reason for her condition. But the mind is a powerful force and she *wishes* to be ill. Oh, not fatally, by any means! But ill enough to worry an unfaithful husband.'

'He doesn't worry,' Olivia said quickly, bitterly.

'Exactly! She's an actress and no doubt he thinks she is playing a part to bring him back, preferably on his knees and begging to be forgiven. She is a possessive woman. She cannot let go. Most important of all, she can't accept the fact that he can live without her. She's a very lovely woman who has been thoroughly spoiled, I'm afraid.' He smiled suddenly, very warm. 'You have all my sympathy. If you were an agency nurse and a stranger, she would be difficult enough to handle. Because she is fond of you and needs you, she doesn't hesitate to give you hell, I expect.'

He was very perceptive, very sensitive to underlying currents. She would need to be very much on her guard if she didn't want this man to sense the strange and disturbing excitement that he generated in her without even trying, Olivia thought ruefully.

'Oh, I don't mind,' she assured him, meaning it. 'She knows I won't leave her while she needs me, of course. I'm much too fond of her. At the moment, she's just a bewildered little girl with a heartache that she doesn't know how to cope with.'

Morgan looked down at the pretty face with so much affectionate concern in the grey eyes. She had integrity as well as warmth of heart and strength of character, he thought with liking and approval.

'Haven't you a life of your own to lead?' he asked quietly.

Olivia understood him. A little warmth crept into her face but she met his gaze without flinching. 'I was engaged to be married until a short time ago,' She told him steadily. 'He changed his mind. So you see, I can sympathise with Celeste. I do know what she feels.'

'And you—coped with your heartache?' he said gently.

Olivia felt her heart tilt in the oddest fashion as she met the warm understanding in those dark eyes. She took instant refuge in levity. 'Oh, I couldn't afford the time for a breakdown, being a busy nurse—and when I had the time, I found I no longer had the inclination!' she declared lightly.

Morgan was moved by her courage, undeceived by the light-hearted tone and the bright smile, and he approved of her philosophical, well-balanced attitude to a disappointment that had obviously gone deep.

'Sensible girl!' he approved, smiling. 'We could use someone like you at the clinic—particularly with your training. When your cousin no longer needs you, perhaps you'll think seriously about joining us?'

Olivia was surprised, rather flattered—and not foolish enough to think that the suggestion was motivated by personal interest. 'Why, yes! Yes, I will think about it,' she promised. 'It would certainly be an interesting change from nursing in a big hospital like Kit's. But I should need to brush up on my French! Jean-Paul says my accent is terrible,' she added, laughing.

His eyes narrowed slightly at the mention of the young Frenchman who was reputed to have a way with women. But he said nothing—and within a few more moments, took his leave.

Olivia found that she needed a little time to quieten her fast-beating heart before she rejoined her cousin on the terrace.

There was the hint of an exciting promise in the depths of those dark, deep-set eyes and he could smile in a way that must threaten even the most level-headed woman's heart if she didn't take care to guard against his charm.

Perhaps it was just as well that she couldn't compete with the very lovely Celeste for his admiration and interest . . .

CHAPTER FOUR

Over the next week, he was very admiring, very interested and very attentive—and Celeste responded to the warmth of his charm and physical magnetism like a flower to the sun.

Olivia couldn't help admiring the doctor's skill and sensitivity and subtle psychology, observing that her cousin was relaxed rather than excited by his attentions. Celeste was friendly rather than flirtatious, content to let the relationship develop at its own pace, unconsciously following his clever and very discreet lead. At the same time, Olivia was sure that his attitude sprang from more than professional interest in his beautiful patient.

To some extent, she welcomed that interest, for it gave her occasional relief from the considerable demands made upon her by her cousin. She was never off duty, day or night, unless Morgan Beauclerc managed to snatch an hour from his busy day to be with Celeste or neglected other friends and interests to spend the evening at the villa. Celeste was more possessive and demanding than she would have dared to be with a stranger, of course. But an agency nurse couldn't have supplied her most important need which was love and understanding rather than medical attention.

Sometimes it was difficult for Olivia to impress on Jean-Paul that she couldn't simply abandon her duties to spend time with him, however attractive the idea. And she was tempted. For she did like him and it would be pleasant to forget Celeste and everything and everyone else for a few hours in his company. He was a dear, so amusing, so attentive, so warm and engaging with his eager friendliness and boyish charm.

He made her laugh and she had forgotten the importance of a shared sense of humour. They liked the same things—and that was important, too. Most important of all, he didn't make her feel that his interest in her was primarily sexual.

She had been surprised to learn that he was a serious musician and a composer who had come to the tiny, secluded village on the Côte d'Azur to work on the score for a musical. She had been right about the guitar, but that was his relaxation, apparently.

He had slipped into the habit of spending most evenings with them. Knowing that Celeste liked his company and that Morgan Beauclerc did not object, Olivia didn't discourage him.

One evening, after an excellent meal and some of the Beaujolais that he had brought as his contribution, Jean-Paul played for them, soft and soothing guitar music of his own composition, just right for their relaxed mood.

Celeste was curled on the sofa, her hand lying lightly on Morgan's arm, her head almost on his shoulder as the music lulled her with its gentle rhythms. They did not seem in the least like doctor and patient, Olivia thought with that recurring twinge of dislike for the rapport that had leapt so swiftly between her cousin and the attractive Morgan Beauclerc. But he was behaving impeccably, she admitted.

He might be falling in love with Celeste like so many men before him, but he did not make it obvious. Olivia suspected that her sensitivity to his feelings sprang from an over-acute awareness of her own where he was concerned.

Lying back in a chair, allowing the music to flow over her, she observed the doctor through half-closed eyes and wondered what it was about him that impressed and attracted her so much.

He was a very handsome man, of course. She liked the way the black hair waved crisply from the temples and nestled in tight curls on the nape of his neck. She thought that any woman might be forgiven for aching to twine her fingers in those curls. She liked the strong good looks with their exciting hint of sensuality. She liked the slow smile that sometimes quickened her heart and sometimes quickened her senses. He was attractive—and dangerous. Because she liked him too much and there was something at the back of her mind that warned her against liking him at all.

Why had he left Kit's in such a hurry all those years ago? Why did she have this vague feeling that he was not to be trusted? And why did she want him so much when he was little more than a stranger?

Olivia was much too honest to deny the clamour of a body that stirred for the merest touch of his hand. She ached for his arms about her, the nearness of him, the potent magic of a kiss that might sweep her beyond all caution.

She told herself levelly that it was only a heady physical attraction but she didn't attempt to dismiss it with contempt. For it was too forceful, too compelling—and really rather frightening that someone as level-headed as herself could respond so easily to a stranger. Never again would she marvel at a girl's inability to keep her head and her virginity, she thought wryly. Meeting Morgan Beauclerc had provided her with a valuable insight even if it never brought satisfaction for that insistent yearning.

Jean-Paul laid aside his guitar. '*Madame dort. . .*' he said softly.

Roused from reverie, Olivia realised with a startled glance that it was true. The lovely head had slipped to rest on Morgan's broad shoulder and the curved lids had drooped to veil the beautiful violet eyes. The rhythm of her breathing and the soft rise and fall of her breast betrayed that she had fallen asleep to the soothing lullaby of Jean-Paul's playing.

Carefully, so gently that his touch might have been a lover's, Morgan eased his position and the slight body so that he could lift Celeste into his arms. She stirred, murmured sleepily, nestled against him like a child who didn't mean to wake.

With Olivia hurrying before him to open doors, to whisk the silk coverlet from the bed, Morgan carried the sleeping girl across the hall and into her bedroom. Glancing back over her shoulder, Olivia saw him touch his lips to the pale cloud of Celeste's shining hair and felt her heart falter in absurd dismay.

Meeting her eyes, Morgan smiled in rueful apology for a very human weakness. Olivia smiled back, careful not to show that she minded although it was impossible to pretend that she hadn't seen that light kiss.

'Most unprofessional, I know,' he murmured, dark eyes twinkling. 'But what man could resist . . . ?'

'Ssh!' Olivia put her finger to her lips in quick warning as the eyelids flickered slightly.

But it was obvious that Celeste wasn't going to wake.

As he placed her gently against the soft pillows, she sighed, slipped deeper into sleep. Morgan took the coverlet from Olivia and spread it over the recumbent figure with an unmistakably tender concern.

Outside the room, he turned to Olivia, smiled. 'What could be better for her? A contented mind induces sleep without the need for pills, you see.' He smoothed his dark hair with his hands. 'She is already making progress, I think.'

Olivia said, a little dryly: 'Your medicine certainly seems to agree with her.'

He looked at her quickly, eyes narrowed with sudden amusement. 'You don't approve?'

'I want her well,' she said firmly, meaning it, suppressing the ridiculous jealousy that threatened her affection and concern for her cousin. 'I don't care how you do it if it works!'

She walked into the sitting-room where Jean-Paul was idly plucking at the strings of his guitar. He looked up with a swift, warm smile for her. 'Listen! I have a new song, just for you . . .' He played the first bars, vibrant and memorable. 'I shall call it '*O for Olivia*' and it will make me a lot of money and I shall dress you in gold and diamonds, *chérie*!'

Morgan paused in the doorway, appraising them both with a faint smile. Jean-Paul had obviously tumbled into love with his usual impetuosity. But this time it might be the real thing. She was a charming girl, pretty and warm-hearted and conscientious. She was courageous, too. She had been hurt and put it behind her and she deserved to be happy. Perhaps the engaging Jean-Paul was just the man to make her happy, he thought, realising that there was already a bond of some kind between them. It showed in the exchange of smiles and glances, the warm understanding underlying the light-hearted banter, the obvious ease of their very new relationship.

Feeling *de trop*, he went away so that they could enjoy the rest of the evening on their own. Jean-Paul was grateful for his tact. Olivia thought it very obvious that the evening had fallen flat for him with Celeste's unplanned retirement to her room.

Alert for the slightest sound of stirring with the ear of a well-trained nurse, Olivia sat with Jean-Paul, talking softly and drinking the last of the wine.

She was fascinated by the account of his struggle to be recognised as a serious composer by the music world who regarded him as a guitarist who only wrote pop music. He told her of the sudden and unexpected break-through when one of his compositions was chosen as the theme music for a film and the string of successes that had followed. He told her about the commission to write the score of a musical play based on the love life of Napoleon. He had left Paris to work through the summer months by the sea that had always been his inspiration.

He drew her to talk about herself, too, and Olivia found herself telling him all about Keith and the promise of marriage that had abruptly come to nothing. Jean-Paul listened and understood and comforted her with a kiss, very tender, his lips soft and warm on her own. It was very easy and very natural to return that gentle and undemanding kiss, she found. He put an arm about her and drew her close and she didn't resist. Why should she? She had nothing to fear from Jean-Paul.

He kissed her again with just a hint of ardour. His

hand hovered and then touched her breast in very tentative caress. Perhaps it was the wine or perhaps she was merely disarmed by that almost-hesitant, almost-innocent approach, but she allowed his hand to curve gently about the mound of her breast as she returned his kiss with affectionate warmth.

She hadn't realised how much she missed the comfort of a man's embrace, the pleasure in a man's kiss, the compliment in a man's attentions, and she didn't feel that there was any danger in encouraging Jean-Paul's gentle and very soothing brand of lovemaking. She knew that she could check him with a word, a single movement, that he would instantly heed. She knew that she could trust him.

Gradually, his kiss became more ardent and more demanding and there was a new urgency in the pressure of his body against her own as he pressed her against the cushions of the sofa. Olivia abruptly realised that his seeking hand had contrived to gain access to the soft flesh beneath the thin, flowing blouse. As he began to caress her with sensual expertise, she thrust him away, unmoved and disliking the intimacy in his touch.

'*Chérie* . . .' he murmured, coaxing, reaching for her again with eager and unmistakable intent. '*Je t'aime* . . .'

Olivia didn't believe him. It was much too soon for him to be declaring that kind of feeling for her, she felt. He was merely roused by physical desire and she was annoyed with herself for having led him on so naively.

Her body resisted him firmly even while she smoothed the fair curls and kissed the tanned cheek, without passion. 'And I like you, Jean-Paul,' she said lightly, deliberately misunderstanding those soft-spoken words. 'We're friends . . .'

He drew back to search the candid grey eyes. Then he shrugged, smiled. 'Not lovers,' he said, accepting defeat.

'No.' It sounded more definite in English, she felt.

'*À demain* . . . ?' he suggested, philosophical.

Olivia shook her head. 'Not tomorrow. Not ever.' She managed to combine finality with a hint of regret for disappointing him. She did like him, very much. She felt that she could become very fond of him, that they could be close friends. But no way did she see them as lovers. She had come close to marrying one man whose embrace left her completely cold and she did not mean to make the mistake again of supposing that a satisfactory relationship could exist between a man and a woman when the wanting was one-sided.

'Never is a long time,' Jean-Paul declared with his engaging smile, proving his excellent command of English. 'And I am an optimist.'

She laughed on a little rush of affection for him. Jean-Paul was much too experienced to think that there was anything more in the way that she looked and laughed and squeezed his hand. But the golden days of summer were before them and he knew all about coaxing a reluctant woman into enjoyment of sexual delight in his arms. He could be patient. And if she was still reluctant . . . *hélas*, but there were plenty of willing women in his world, he had always found . . .

He left her with a fleeting kiss that a brother or an uncle might have bestowed. Reassured, Olivia watched him walk across the sand towards his own villa, guitar slung over his shoulder, and waved as he turned to wave a last goodnight.

'Where is everyone . . . ?' Celeste was querulous that the evening had ended so absurdly for her. It was undignified to have fallen asleep like an exhausted child at a party, to have been put to bed and left while everyone else continued to enjoy themselves, she declared crossly.

Olivia quickly pointed out that the doctor had left immediately. '*You* were the attraction,' she added lightly, able to sound convincing because she believed it. 'He didn't mean to stay to be bored by Jean-Paul and myself, naturally.'

Celeste yawned delicately, lifted the mass of her hair from her neck with both hands. 'He does like me, don't you think?' she said with a little satisfaction. 'It *is* more than a professional interest?'

Recalling the tender way he had held her beautiful cousin against his breast, touched the soft, shining hair with his lips in almost reverent tenderness, Olivia agreed with a smile that bravely concealed a lingering dismay.

She coaxed Celeste out of her clothes and into a bath, applied the recommended massage that her cousin seemed to find so soothing, gave her a hot drink and a sleeping pill and finally settled her for the night.

It was almost one o'clock but the thought of her own bed didn't tempt her at all. Stimulated by the wine and the events of the evening, Olivia went out to the terrace for a last look at the sea.

She leaned against the low wall and felt the soft breeze tug at her hair and cool her cheeks, the very peace and beauty of the night slowly filter into an oddly troubled heart and mind.

The moon was hiding behind an enormous bank of dark cloud and the sea was just a black mass of uninviting water beyond the shore. In the distance, she saw the lights shining from Jean-Paul's white-washed little house and wondered if he was forgetting his disappointment in work. She fancied she could hear the faint strains of music on the still air. But it was only fancy, she knew.

Dear Jean-Paul. Eager and impulsive and hot-blooded, had he really expected to seduce her so easily with the risk that Celeste might wake and walk in on them at any moment? Honest with herself, Olivia knew that it was a consideration that hadn't weighed with her at the time. She just hadn't felt the least degree of desire for him. She really did regard him as a dear friend rather than a potential lover.

Perhaps it would have been a very different end to the evening if it had been Jean-Paul who went away and Morgan who had remained to make love to her, she thought, rather ruefully—and a delicate sigh of a shudder unexpectedly swept her from head to toe at the thought of his kiss, his hands on her body in slow and sensual caress.

Briskly, she shook off the absurd longing for a man who scarcely knew she existed except as a capable nurse who cared about her patient. As a doctor, he saw her as a highly-trained nurse who would be a valuable asset to the clinic that he ran with his brother in the nearby town. But as a man he only had eyes for the lovely and enchanting and incomparable Celeste—and who could blame him?

Olivia told herself firmly that she ought to be thankful

that Celeste was beginning to show some interest in a man other than Tom Knight at last. It was something to be approved and encouraged. It was the first step on the road to her complete recovery . . . not only from the breakdown in health but also from loving a man who just didn't care about her at all!

The next morning, Jean-Paul ran across the sand to join them, stocky and muscular and very tanned in the brief scarlet slip that was his only garment. Water glistened on his blond curls and his good-looking and very boyish face glowed from the exertion of his swim.

He threw himself down beside the colourful beach-chairs, panting slightly, greeting them both with his warm and very engaging smile and teasing them lightly about their energetic approach to the day.

'We may look lazy but we were in the water when you were probably still in bed,' Olivia returned brightly, smiling at him. She had noticed the swift appreciation of her cousin's lovely body, considerably exposed by the miniscule black bikini. Her own more modest one-piece swimsuit flattered her figure, too. But men always went for the obvious, she thought with indulgent amusement.

It was so hot that Celeste had suggested a swim. Remembering a certain doctor's instructions, Olivia had swept her down to the sea before she could change her mind. The water had been deliciously warm and very inviting. But she hadn't allowed Celeste to stay in it too long, mindful of how easily she tired.

Now, she was pleased to see Jean-Paul and a little relieved that he didn't seem to bear any grudge for his rebuff of the previous evening. But she hoped he wouldn't tempt Celeste into another swim.

He didn't. But he did suggest that they should both go

sailing with him that afternoon. Rather to her surprise, because her cousin had never cared for boats, Celeste accepted readily.

It was a perfect afternoon for a sail and, being Saturday, there were several other boat-owners who took advantage of the weekend and the weather to take out their vessels.

Celeste lay on a mound of cushions, trailing her fingers in the water, half-asleep beneath an enormous hat that shaded her perfect face, a white silk trouser suit protecting her body from too much sun.

Olivia knew a little about sailing and loved it. Happily, she obeyed the captain's instructions, clambering about the small boat and dodging the boom as it swung back and forth. She looked lithe and lovely in jeans rolled to the knees and a thin shirt that clung more revealingly than she knew to firm young breasts after she had been soaked by flying spray.

She felt about fifteen and looked it, curls whipped in the wind and pretty face glowing with delight. For more than an hour, she forgot everything else to revel in the unexpected and enjoyable adventure in Jean-Paul's company.

On their way back to the jetty, under cover of the big sail, he leaned forward to kiss her—and Olivia threw her arms impulsively about his neck and kissed him back in warmly affectionate gratitude for a lovely afternoon.

A slightly startled expression leaped to the blue eyes. '*Chérie* . . .' he said, very soft.

She smiled uncertainly, troubled by a certain meaningful note in his pleasant voice. She didn't want the complication of serious involvement on his part. She didn't want him to be hurt.

The small boat began to rock in the swell from a speeding motor-launch that came close to them in passing and she suddenly clung to him, laughing.

'*Merci, m'sieu* . . . !' he shouted after the fast boat, eyes dancing, lightening a suddenly tense moment with his air of mischief.

The launch was moored to the wooden jetty by the time they neared it and the owner stood beside it, regarding them with some amusement.

'It's Beauclerc,' Jean-Paul said carelessly, waving to him in friendly fashion.

Celeste sat up and took notice, brightening at sight of the tall figure, casually dressed in jeans and open-necked shirt, his dark hair ruffled by the wind. Olivia felt her heart thump and then she carefully busied herself with helping Jean-Paul to bring the boat round to its mooring-post so that she didn't have to look at him.

But she was compelled to take his strong and very steady hand as he reached to help her from the boat and on to the jetty. Olivia smiled her thanks, suddenly and stupidly shy, suddenly very conscious of the clinging shirt and the fact that she wasn't wearing anything beneath it. But if he noticed the lovely curve of her breasts and the taut nipples thrusting against the cheesecloth, nothing flickered in his dark eyes. Olivia was torn between relief and chagrin.

He was already looking beyond her with obvious surprise to Celeste, risen from her cushions and holding with both hands to the hat that threatened to be whipped away by the little wind that had sprung up. She looked very beautiful, smiling at him.

Olivia choked back a very foolish dismay.

He gave his hand to Celeste. 'This is real progress!' he

declared, delighted. 'I saw Jean-Paul and Miss Paine. I thought you must be resting!'

'What could be more restful than lying in a boat with a gentle sea lapping against the sides?' she countered brightly. 'I have been very lazy and allowed Olivia to do all the work.'

Jean-Paul slid an arm about Olivia's waist and said warmly: 'She is a very good *seconde*!'

Strangely comforted, she leaned against his broad chest, smiling up at him. 'I only swept you into the sea twice with the boom,' she agreed, eyes dancing.

He shrugged, laughed. 'I am a very good swimmer, after all. Fortunately, we have no sharks in the bay. Now we will adjourn to my house for the English habit of afternoon tea. It is arranged.' He turned to the tall doctor with his easy friendliness. 'I hope you will join us?'

'*Avec plaisir, mon ami*!' he said promptly.

Celeste smiled her approval and slipped her hand into his arm with a delicately proprietary air so that no one should be in any doubt that he had accepted the invitation for the sake of her company.

'Perhaps we should go ahead?' Olivia suggested, a little abruptly, addressing Jean-Paul. 'You ought to change out of those wet clothes as quickly as possible. They must be very uncomfortable.'

'It's good advice,' Morgan volunteered lightly. 'Mrs Knight and I will follow at her pace.' He covered the slender hand lying on his arm and smiled down at Celeste.

Like a lover, Olivia thought, running down the wooden steps of the jetty and turning to cross the beach at Jean-Paul's side.

Suddenly he reached for her hand and clasped it firmly. She wondered if he sensed her slight heaviness of heart and hoped he didn't also sense the reason for it. It was almost too foolish to admit to herself, she thought ruefully.

She squeezed Jean-Paul's hand in swift, warm response, smiled at him, forced herself not to think about the way that Morgan Beauclerc had looked and smiled at her beautiful cousin . . .

CHAPTER FIVE

JEAN-PAUL'S villa was very modern in design and decor and strikingly furnished with its deep brown carpets and pale cream furniture. The sitting room was dominated by a grand piano and some *avant-garde* paintings, mostly nudes. One of them was a self-portrait that he remarked on so unselfconsciously that Olivia felt she was prudish and old-fashioned to be slightly embarrassed. After all, she was a nurse and the male body held no mysteries for her. But she still blushed.

He went off to change into dry clothes, leaving her to wander about the room and examine some of his treasures. Her thin shirt had dried as they walked from the jetty in the hot sun and she smilingly shook her head to the offer of one of his shirts.

She was very conscious of her faded jeans and crumpled shirt in comparison with her cousin's cool elegance. She thought there was a faint amusement in Morgan Beauclerc's dark eyes as she turned from the study of Jean-Paul's collection of porcelain on their arrival, some minutes later. She supposed she *was* in vivid contrast to the lovely room and the exquisite china, she thought wryly. But her chin went up just a fraction before his gaze and he looked away.

Jean-Paul returned and tea was served by an elderly and obviously disapproving housekeeper. She was, he explained, a legacy from the previous owner of the villa and he didn't have the heart to get rid of her. At least, she didn't distract him from his work!

Later, Celeste was in excellent spirits, revived by the tea and stimulated by admiration and attention. She sat down at the piano and entertained them with a clever mimicry of a famous French singer that particularly delighted Jean-Paul. She went on to sing one or two songs in her own attractively husky voice and Jean-Paul brought his guitar and strummed an accompaniment. Soon, he was teaching her his latest composition.

Olivia and the doctor were both forgotten, temporarily. She smiled at him with a hint of apology for her cousin who was like a child, easily excited, swift to drop the old and pick up the new as it suited her mood. For the moment, no one existed but the talented young musician who belonged to her particular world—and it was a world that she missed very much, after all.

Morgan moved across the room to sit beside Olivia on the cream leather sofa. Celeste did not even glance in their direction, too absorbed in listening. Jean-Paul's fair head was bent over his guitar as he sang, softly and well. The new song was called *Ballad for a Beautiful Woman* and the intent expression in Celeste's lovely eyes betrayed that she took his singing of the song for her as a compliment.

'I wish I'd known that Jean-Paul was taking you out on his boat,' Morgan said lightly, low so that their conversation did not disturb the others. 'I'd have arranged to spend the afternoon with your cousin so that you could really relax and enjoy yourself. Even the most caring nurse needs a break from her work on occasions.'

It crossed Olivia's mind that he was tacitly approving her friendship with the Frenchman with his words. Perhaps he felt that Jean-Paul's attentions would be beneficial to her recovery from a broken engagement while he applied himself to the pleasurable task of curing Celeste's heartache, she thought dryly, unaccountably irritated.

'It's a kind thought,' she returned coolly, without gratitude. 'But even the most caring doctor needs to forget all about his patients for a few hours on occasions. You are obviously off duty this afternoon, Dr Beauclerc.'

He smiled at the way she had used his own words against him. 'So are you.' His smile deepened to sudden, enchanting warmth. 'No uniform and no badge, I notice. So there really isn't any reason why we should be so rigidly formal. Just call me Morgan.'

It was nothing more than friendliness, Olivia told herself, having to be very firm with the heart that leaped so foolishly at the warmth in eyes and voice and smile of a very attractive man. She was much too aware of him, pulses quickening and the beginnings of desire stirring in the secret places of her body at the very nearness of him.

'For heaven's sake, don't call me Olivia!' she forestalled him quickly, anxiously. 'Celeste would be furious!'

'If I do, she won't hear me,' he assured her, amused. 'I hope I'm not so tactless! But it's quite ridiculous to go on calling you Nurse or Miss Paine with every other word, don't you think? So archaic! If we were both at Kit's, we'd be on first-name terms out of hearing of the patients.'

'If we were both at Kit's, I doubt if we'd have much to do with each other, on or off the ward,' she returned carefully, meaning that he would never notice anyone as ordinary as herself. She had known too many doctors like this one, too attractive for their own good or anyone else's, always in pursuit of one conquest or another. She had never attracted the attention of his type—or wanted to do so. She had always preferred the Keiths, easy to know and like, reliable and trustworthy and loyal.

He moved with sudden impatience. 'Give a dog a bad name . . . !' he exclaimed sharply. 'I'm sorry that you should judge me on the strength of those old stories—*and* surprised! You seem such a fair-minded girl!'

Olivia was slightly taken aback. 'That isn't what I meant,' she said defensively and with truth. 'I don't know any stories about you. None that I can remember, anyway! You left Kit's almost as soon as I began my training!'

'I'm sorry . . .' Contrite, he covered her hand with his strong fingers and smiled ruefully. 'I'm still rather sensitive about those days, obviously.'

His touch did strange things to her, tumbling her heart and vibrating her senses, shooting a quiver of excitement along her spine and sending an absurd rush of tears to prick at her eyes.

Abruptly, she drew away her hand before it was tempted to curve and cling to those warm fingers. 'Whatever you did really doesn't interest me,' she said firmly, so anxious to appear indifferent in case he realised her growing involvement that she spoke more coldly than she knew.

'Whatever *I* did . . . !' He broke off, hearing the shaft of anger invade his tone. He was silent, struggling with a familiar bitterness and a novel kind of disappointment. Then he said, very quietly: 'You're quite right, of course. The past has nothing to do with the present, Miss Paine. Forgive me for assuming that a common bond with Kit's gave me some kind of right to your friendship.'

He got to his feet and walked across the room to stand by the piano, praising song and singer as Jean-Paul struck the final chords and smiling at Celeste as she turned eagerly to him.

Celeste brushed a hand across wet eyes. 'I hate songs that make me cry!' she exclaimed, between tears and laughter.

Jean-Paul slid the strap of his guitar from his shoulder. 'Tears wash the dust from the eyes, *Madame*,' he said gently, the warmth in his pleasant voice taking the formal title and turning it into an expression of affection.

She looked at him quickly, suspicious and hostile. 'Livvy talks too much!'

Jean-Paul shook his fair head and smiled. He had a very sweet, rather boyish smile that was quite irresistible. 'Olivia tells me nothing. The way you look when I am singing my song tells me everything,' he replied smoothly. 'I am a musician . . . It is my business to make music that opens up the heart.'

Celeste put her hand on his arm. 'It was a lovely song. Don't sing it again—not to me. Now I think that Livvy and I should go home. I'm very tired . . .'

Olivia pulled herself together, glad of the little bustle of departure that made it unnecessary for her actually to exchange any more words with Morgan Beauclerc. Celeste did enough talking for both of them, over-excited by the events of the day. Olivia was glad to be quiet as they walked the short distance between the villas. The dismissive words of a proud man were still echoing in her ears, disturbing and puzzling. She hadn't felt that he liked her very much or regarded her as anything but a nurse in charge of one of his patients. Yet he had spoken as though it had mattered to him that they should be friends. And she had offended him without even knowing *how*! Which made it impossible for her to apologise, she thought wryly . . .

Having been in a good mood for most of the day, Celeste abruptly decided to be difficult. She wasn't hungry, she said, pushing away her plate. She was bored. She didn't want to read or to watch television or listen to music or play backgammon. She wasn't an old lady! No, she was damned if she'd go tamely to bed with a sleeping pill at a time when everyone else was setting out to enjoy themselves at theatre or nightclub or party! No one cared that she felt so ill—not even Livvy who had come to take care of her and not to flirt with every man in sight!

'What were you whispering about on the sofa with Morgan, anyway?' she demanded angrily. 'Secrets? Arranging to meet him? Well, I can't allow you to leave me for hours on end while you enjoy yourself. I'm sorry!'

'We were only talking about Kit's . . .' She could have bitten out her tongue as soon as the words left her lips. For Celeste seized on them as if she had been lying in wait for an admission that they had something in common that excluded her.

'Kit's? What about Kit's? Is that where he trained? Did you know him, then? You didn't say! How very sly!'

Olivia held on to her patience with both hands, resenting the suspicion and the animosity in her cousin's hard voice and knowing that she must swallow it.

'I don't know where he trained,' she said firmly and with truth. 'He just happened to be a doctor at Kit's when I went there as a very green junior.'

'Then you *did* know him!'

'No. Only by name.' She was careful not to add *and by*

reputation. 'He was a registrar. Does it matter, Celeste? He wasn't and isn't interested in me, I promise you! Heavens, you know very little about hospital hierarchy if you think that a registrar would take the least notice of a first-year nurse! They are less than the dust to senior doctors,' she added lightly.

Celeste looked at her with narrowed eyes. 'But you aren't a first-year now—and he isn't a hospital registrar. You're doctor and nurse with a mutual interest—me! That gives you plenty of opportunity to meet and talk and how do I know that you're innocently discussing my health every time you go into a huddle?'

Olivia supposed she should be pleased that Celeste cared enough to be rather jealous. It was a healthy sign that she liked Morgan Beauclerc and found him attractive, no doubt. It showed that she was no longer quite so obsessed with thoughts of Tom and the past. But she couldn't feel happy about it.

She tried to tell herself that she was just concerned for Celeste who couldn't afford to be hurt all over again by any man. At Kit's, he had earned himself a reputation as a rake, justified or not, and he had certainly been involved in a scandal of some kind. Now, he was taking a very unprofessional degree of interest in a patient and it might be most unwise of Celeste to be so encouraging.

It was all quite true. But Olivia was honest enough to admit that she was much more concerned with the impact on her own emotions of a too-attractive man that she might never have met if he hadn't happened to be a doctor, too.

'You *don't* know,' she said, slightly sharp. 'You'll just have to take my word for it, won't you?'

Celeste crumpled like a child. 'Oh, I'm sorry,' she said

penitently. 'I don't know why I'm being so spiteful. Of course there's nothing going on between you. That's obvious. He isn't your type at all and I don't suppose he's even noticed that you're quite a pretty girl.'

Damned with faint praise, Olivia thought dryly. 'Whoever sees the moon when the sun is in the sky?' she countered lightly, affectionately teasing but knowing it to be true. What man had ever looked at her twice when the delicately lovely Celeste was around? She was too used to it to mind, she told herself firmly, ignoring a twinge of regret that Morgan Beauclerc should be as dazzled by her cousin as all the others. 'He only has eyes for you, darling. Very flattering!'

'Oh, I'm just another patient,' Celeste demurred, patently not believing it.

'And I'm just another nurse.' Olivia smiled at her. 'So why don't we both forget all about Dr Beauclerc for tonight and get you tucked into bed so that you're looking your best when he sees you again. We don't want any shadows beneath those beautiful eyes, do we?'

It was absurd but it worked. Sometimes Olivia wondered if her cousin was slipping back to childish behaviour and attitudes as an escape from the hurtful reality of maturity. She hated to use such tactics with someone she loved and had always admired for her intelligence as well as beauty. It was sad that they were necessary because they were effective.

She sank into a chair in the spacious and pleasant sitting-room, having finally settled her troublesome patient for the first part of the night, at least.

Now, she was free to relax, to spend the rest of the evening as she wished, she thought, a little dryly. She could read or watch television or listen to music or play patience—or simply catch up on her own beauty sleep! She did not expect to see Jean-Paul for he was busy with friends that evening, she knew.

She felt a certain sympathy with Celeste's frustration at the lack of a full social life in this quiet coastal village. Her own social life had never been terribly exciting but she had enjoyed it. Suddenly she missed the company and the conversation of her many friends at Kit's. Suddenly she missed Keith, too—the comfort of his affection and concern and liking for her company, if nothing else!

Olivia sighed and reached for one of the glossy and sophisticated magazines that reflected a way of life that she was never likely to know and did not envy.

'How is Madame?'

The sound of Jean-Paul's voice startled her, speaking from the terrace. The long window was never closed until everyone retired for the night. Then Marthe went around locking doors and windows against intruders although the village had a reputation for being remarkably free of crime of every description.

'What are you doing here?' Startled, she spoke more sharply than she knew.

He stiffened. 'I'm sorry if I intrude.'

He was very sensitive, Olivia thought, seeing the flicker of hurt in his eyes. She held out her hand, smiling, repentant. 'Sorry, Jean-Paul! It's just that you took me by surprise. I didn't expect you.'

His eyes narrowed. 'You are expecting someone else?'

She shook her head, laughed. 'Of course not! Come in and talk to me . . .' she invited warmly, glad of some company.

He took her hand and carried it to his lips, kissing it lightly. 'I came to enquire about Madame.' It had become his name for Celeste, more affectionate than respectful. 'It was a day very exciting for her, *n'est ce pas*? She was so tired. If I stay, I shall make love to you, *chérie*,' he added abruptly, an almost rueful smile in his eyes as he looked down at her.

Olivia drew him down to sit beside her, suddenly needing an ease for the dreadful ache of loneliness deep down inside. 'Then stay,' she said impulsively, rather recklessly, smiling on him with affection. She wanted the forgetfulness that she might find in his arms, she decided abruptly . . . something to blot out the haunting image of another man's face in her mind's eye, to erase the tormenting memory of another man's touch and what it could do to her weak and very wanton body. She put her arms about Jean-Paul, kissed him. His lips were warm and very sweet and surprisingly unresponsive. She drew away, searched his eyes with a mingled dismay and relief.

He touched his hand to her cheek. 'What is it, *chérie*? Have you been thinking of your Keith?' he asked quietly.

He was too perceptive, too sensitive—and it was nice of him not to mind that she had been trying to use him as a substitute. She was thankful that he didn't know that it was not Keith but another and very different man who evoked that strange, sad wanting within her being.

She smiled wryly. 'Perhaps . . . a little.' It was true. There was no need to add that she had been thinking of Morgan Beauclerc . . . a lot!

The telephone rang. She rose quickly and went to answer before the shrill summons roused Celeste.

'Olivia?'

'Yes.' She was cautious, not immediately recognising the deep voice. Then she did—and her heart leaped into her throat with quite unfounded hope.

'Tell me, do you have any experience of theatre work?' he asked without preliminary. 'Other than the routine training, I mean?'

'Yes, I do.' She was surprised but swift to reassure him. 'I worked for six months as Theatre Staff Nurse last year.'

'Good girl,' he said briskly. 'I've an emergency here . . . a child with intestinal blockage. I want you to assist. My theatre nurse is ill and it will take too long to arrange for someone else to stand in. Come right away, will you? I'll send a car for you.'

'No need. Jean-Paul is with me and I know he'll drive me to the clinic.' She glanced at the Frenchman and he sent her a confirming nod. She smiled gratefully. 'I'll be with you as soon as possible,' she said firmly. She didn't hesitate. She was a trained nurse and a child was in urgent need of surgery.

Jean-Paul was already moving towards the door. 'I'll get my car and be back for you in five minutes, Olivia . . . !'

She went to find Marthe, to explain and ask the housekeeper to listen for Celeste who might wake and call at any time. Marthe was to tell her what had happened. She was needed urgently at the Beauclerc Clinic and would be back as soon as possible.

She wondered if she had managed to make the woman understand with her stumbling schoolgirl French but there was no time to worry about it. She heard the screech of the brakes of Jean-Paul's car as he swung into the drive and halted and she ran out to join him.

She hadn't changed from her cool linen frock, worn for dinner. There was little need because she would soon be donning surgical gown and scrubbing-up to assist in the theatre. She was grateful for that six months at Kit's which had given her valuable experience of almost every kind of surgery.

Morgan was waiting for her in the reception area, tense and slightly impatient. Olivia had no time to notice or admire the lay-out of the clinic, founded and run by Gerard Beauclerc.

Morgan came to meet her, thanked and dismissed Jean-Paul with a rapid flow of French and very little ceremony, and then swept her off to the top floor operating theatre by way of the lift.

On the way, he explained that he intended to create an opening between part of the small intestine and the sigmoid flexure of the colon. Known as an ileosigmoidostomy, it was a delicate and difficult operation when it involved a three-day-old baby, as in this case. Olivia didn't doubt that he was equal to it. She only hoped that she wouldn't fail him at a vital moment and she racked her brains to remember the correct procedure as she began to scrub-up in the ante-room.

All her nervousness evaporated as she stood beside him beneath the bright arc lights of the theatre, slender figure enveloped in the green surgical gown and bright hair concealed by the loose cap, grey eyes alert for every step of the operation above the green mask. The anaesthetised infant was brought in on a trolley and transferred to the table.

Morgan waited for the anaesthetist's nod to proceed. There was a few moments of fiddling with taps and tubes before it came. Olivia could sense the tension in the tall, silent man who stood by her side, flexing his clever hands in the thin surgical gloves.

The nod came. He drew a deep breath and straightened his broad shoulders, held out a hand. 'Right,' he said carefully. 'Scalpel, please, Nurse . . .'

It was instantly slapped into his hand and he nodded approval, the hint of a smile for Olivia in the dark eyes. But it was the last time during the operative procedure that he showed the slightest awareness of her as anything but an efficient robot who passed instruments and supplied swabs with cool precision and automatic reflex.

It was a lengthy operation, demanding complete and tireless concentration. When it was finally over, he stepped back from the table and the brilliant lights while the anaesthetist busied himself with his mass of equipment. Then the theatre staff gently transferred the unconscious infant to a trolley and wheeled him off to the recovery room and Morgan visibly relaxed. He pulled down his mask and smiled at Olivia with the sudden euphoria of a tired man who knew that he had successfully tackled a difficult job.

Olivia suddenly realised that she was almost dropping with fatigue. The heat from the arc lights, the inability to relax even for a second, the tension of willing him to do well had all taken their toll. She was emotionally rather than physically drained. She smiled back at him, weary but very glad that she had been useful, conscious that they shared a new rapport that nothing and no-one could threaten. The life of a child had hung in the balance and between them they had tilted the scales towards an optimistic prognosis.

'There's nothing like a Kit's nurse at times like these,'

he said warmly. 'I'm really very grateful to you, Miss Paine.'

She felt a tiny stab of dismay at the formality that seemed to set up the former barrier between them. 'It was *Olivia* when you telephoned,' she said impulsively. very light.

He raised an amused eyebrow. 'Was it? A dreadful slip of the tongue,' he declared, teasing her. 'I'm sure you are much too well-trained to forget to call me anything but Dr Beauclerc!'

She laughed as she met the engaging smile in his eyes, warming to him. At the very back of her mind might be the lingering of mistrust but he had a great deal of charm and he was very attractive, very personable. 'Oh, very well—but *pas devant ma cousine*!'

'I'll remember,' he promised, smiling at her with a conspiratorial twinkle. 'Now, go and take off those shapeless garments and turn back into a woman and I'll give you some coffee before I take you back to the Villa Paradis.'

It was very late—or, rather, very early. The villa would be wrapped in sleep and she hoped that her cousin had been sleeping so soundly that she hadn't even discovered that Olivia had been out for those few hours.

Stimulated rather than tired, she did not want to go tamely back to the villa and bed. She might never have another opportunity to be with Morgan Beauclerc without Celeste breathing down her neck and she was very tempted to make the most of the mood and the moment.

She splashed her face with cold water, ran her fingers through her thick curls in lieu of a comb and went to join the waiting doctor.

She was a little surprised but she didn't demur when

he suggested that they should enjoy their coffee in the privacy of his flat—but her heart began to beat rather fast . . .

CHAPTER SIX

MORGAN'S private flat was situated in a separate wing of the clinic. While he made coffee in the small and very neat kitchen, Olivia wandered about his sitting-room, taking an interest in his possessions.

Books, pictures, taste in music—the kind of things that a man gathered about him in his home were indications of his character and personality, she felt. This was a very masculine abode, convincing her that the only women in his life were those with whom he enjoyed brief and sensual encounters.

She was pleased to find some of her own favourites among his books. She turned to say so and found him regarding her with an oddly disturbing smile in his eyes—and her heart missed a beat. The light, unimportant words died on her lips.

She knew instinctively that he wanted her with all the urgent and compelling passion of an ardent man. Perhaps he sensed the excitement that he evoked in her without even trying. Or perhaps he simply responded to any woman who was reasonably young and reasonably pretty. However it was, the glow in his dark eyes was quite unmistakable and so was the tension in his tall body.

'Olivia . . .' he said unsteadily, achingly.

Blindly following her instincts, without a thought for the consequences, she moved into his arms.

His kiss, urgent yet tender, held all the magic that she

had dreamed it would. His body was taut, throbbing with passion, echoing the fierce drum-beat of desire in her slender frame. Her heart was drumming a similar tattoo, high in her throat. The blood tingled in her veins with an all-consuming fire and her body was so weak with wanting that she needed his strong arms about her for support.

He kissed her with very sensual ardour and Olivia clung to him, trembling, her heart pounding, knowing that she wanted him as she had never wanted any man before. Her body clamoured for him with a tumult of excitement and she was ready to drown in the ecstatic sea of his lovemaking.

She didn't doubt that he wanted her, too. He held her very close, crushing her soft breasts against him, and there was a kind of hunger in his embrace that every part of her being yearned to satisfy.

Suddenly, without warning, he put her away from him . . . so abruptly that Olivia had to reach her hand to the back of a chair to steady herself. He smiled at her with an understanding that she didn't welcome. Wanting him so desperately was one thing, having him know it was quite another.

Morgan wondered why he had clamped that iron control on his passions all in a moment. He needed the release from the night's tensions that he could find in her arms. But there was something about this girl with her warmth of heart and sweetness of nature and shining integrity that made him pause to wonder if he could take her and forget her as easily as all those other conquests of his past.

He was shaken by the warm and eager and very generous response. He was startled by an unrealised depth to his liking for this young and caring nurse. And, suspecting that she was a virgin, he was surprised that she had turned into his arms and welcomed his kiss as though she had been waiting for it all week and didn't care where it might lead her.

Proud, slightly on the defensive because she knew she had been too encouraging, afraid of betraying the turmoil of heart and body, Olivia took refuge in levity. She didn't want him to suspect that his kiss had made such an impact on her emotions.

'Whatever happened to the coffee?' she asked lightly. 'I shall begin to think that you lured me here on false pretences!'

Morgan smiled at her, very warm. 'And who could blame me?' he returned, equally light. 'You're a very attractive girl!'

'Celeste for one! As it is, she'll want to know where I've been all these hours,' she declared, wryly.

Morgan went into the kitchen and returned with a tray. 'Does it require an explanation? Other than the obvious fact that a complicated operation takes a considerable amount of time.'

'Celeste knows nothing about surgery or its procedures,' she pointed out. 'She's going to take some convincing, I'm afraid.' Thinking of her cousin's inevitable suspicions about the hours she had spent with the doctor, her tone was rueful.

Morgan poured coffee, steaming, fragrant. 'But it isn't really her concern, is it?' he said gently. 'And if you spent the night with me there isn't a thing she could do about it!'

Olivia's heart jumped. She looked at him quickly, wondering if it was an invitation—and decided that it wasn't as she met the reassurance in his slightly smiling eyes. Her heart steadied. 'She'd *say* a lot!' she exclaimed, laughing. 'And she'd probably book a seat on the first plane back to England for me!'

'That would be a very great pity,' he said, softly, with meaning.

Colour stole into her face. Their hands brushed as she took the proffered cup and his touch seemed to vibrate throughout her body. Her smile wavered at the shock of that physical contact.

She sipped her coffee. 'I needed this,' she said with feeling.

Their eyes met and held. The atmosphere was suddenly tense, electric. 'I need *you*, Olivia,' he said, very direct.

The urgency of his need communicated itself to her, sent that arrow of desire shafting into the innermost depths of her slender and very vulnerable body. Her hand trembled as she set the cup into its saucer and put both down on the low table. 'Please . . . take me back now,' she said unsteadily. She got to her feet.

So did he. They stood looking at each other, a hint of a plea in her wide grey eyes and naked need in the dark eyes that looked back at her. She knew that he was just as aware of the flame burning so bright in her as she was of his fierce and almost frightening desire.

He put his hands to her shoulders and drew her slowly towards him and Olivia didn't resist. She couldn't. There was an almost-hypnotic magnetism in his smile, his gaze, his touch. He touched his lips to her hair, her temple, her cheek, trailing a route to the warm and swiftly welcoming mouth while his fingers were busy with the buttons of her frock. With his mouth hard and urgent on her own, she allowed him to slide the material from her shoulders and run his hands over their bare smoothness. She felt his touch at the swell of her breasts. His kiss soothed and reassured the quiver of alarm, swayed her senses as he unclipped the flimsy bra to release the small breasts from their confinement. Her body arched against him on a slight sigh. Morgan held her away to study her nude loveliness and caught his breath in swift admiration. Heart pounding, body on fire for him, Oliva smiled at him in unconscious surrender.

He bent his head to kiss her taut breasts in homage and felt her tremble as his lips nuzzled the sensitive aureoles of her nipples. With a suddenly swift and decisive movement, he lifted her into his arms and kissed her with an urgency that left her in no doubt of the outcome.

He carried her into the bedroom and laid her gently against the pillows and Olivia held out her arms to him on a sigh, wanting him, wanting desperately to know what awaited her in that mysterious world to which he held the key.

Morgan stripped out of his clothes and bent to kiss her once more in a way that roused her to greater heights of sexual desire even before she felt his hands on her body or knew his descending weight.

Her body moved to meet him, eagerly. She welcomed him as a lover without hesitation, recognising him as the one man she had been destined to know and to love.

Their bodies fused and she melted in that fierce flame of passion. Nothing had prepared her for the breathless and magical world of delight that she found in his arms. He was a skilled and sensitive lover, infinitely tender, ardently passionate and yet incredibly patient, knowing just how to please and delight her and coax her towards the ultimate glory, carrying her with him to the towering peaks of ecstasy and beyond.

Her long, shuddering sigh broke the spell of enchantment that had bound them both. Slowly and reluctantly, they came back to earth. Spent, he lay by her side, an arm outflung across her naked breasts. He turned his head to kiss her, very gently. Olivia put a hand to his head, thrust her fingers into the thick black curls just as she had longed to do since the first moment of meeting.

I love you, trembled on her lips, welling from her heart.

He kissed her again before she could voice the heartfelt words and she wondered if he had sensed what was quivering on her lips—and didn't want to hear it.

Perhaps it had been too often and too easily said to him by other women in the golden aftermath of lovemaking, she thought heavily. He could not know that it was so entirely the truth, that she would love him until the end of time. And why should he believe it when she could scarcely believe it herself? They were still strangers, after all. Becoming lovers all in a moment didn't alter the fact that it was only a matter of days since they had met for the first time.

'*Sweet* . . .' he murmured softly, very tender.

Tears, unbidden, suddenly pressed against her eyes. She closed them, forcing back that rush of pain and disappointment.

Morgan raised himself on an elbow and looked at the lovely, slightly troubled face. He kissed the soft, quivering eyelids, one after the other, and tasted salt. He drew her into his arms. 'Regrets?' His question was very gentle, very understanding.

Olivia shook her head. She put her arms about him and held him very tightly, not caring that his hard body bruised her soft and tender breasts with the fierce strength of her embrace. 'No!' she said, very firm.

He smiled wryly. She had been a virgin. Knowing it, he had still taken her on that storm of exciting and utterly irresistible passion—and she had given with a wealth of generosity that had made it the most memorable of sexual experiences. There had been many women, most of them forgotten, none of them very important. He knew that he would never forget Olivia. He suspected that she was destined to become very important in his life. At the same time, he still hesitated to commit himself irrevocably to any woman—even one as enchanting and as appealing as this one.

'I'm glad it was good for you,' he said warmly. 'Sometimes it isn't—the first time.' He brushed a strand of soft hair from her eyes, smiled into them. 'Don't they have red-blooded men at Kit's any more?' he teased, lightening the moment, kindly laughter lurking in the dark eyes. 'It was different in my day!'

'I'm an old-fashioned girl,' Olivia returned, carefully light. 'I was saving myself for the man I meant to marry. Now I wonder why!' She felt it might be better if he supposed that she had surrendered that valued virginity out of a sudden bitterness with the shattered hopes and dreams of the past rather than because she had fallen headlong and hopelessly in love with him in the present. She might have lost both heart and virginity to him. She could still hang on to her pride, she thought ruefully.

'Does it still hurt so much?' he asked, rather abruptly.

'No.'

Morgan didn't believe that quick, defensive monosyllable. He felt sudden dislike of her lingering feeling for that other man, but he knew instinctively that a genuine and very honest passion had sent her into his arms, so he could not really be jealous of the shadowy figure from her past. Instead, he despised the man for a fool who had turned away something of very great value. Scarcely knowing Olivia, he was still sure that she had much to give and that a man should count himself fortunate if she loved him.

He knew that he should rouse himself, dress and drive her to the Villa Paradis so that she could have a few hours of sleep before the start of another demanding day. But he didn't want to part with her when it seemed so right and natural for her to be in his arms, warm and yielding and lovely—and so desirable that his body stirred with new desire.

He kissed her, touched her breast like a lover, and she turned to him in swift response. Again they made love, slowly and sensuously, discovering further delight in each other, and then drifted into sleep, still entwined and utterly content.

The sun woke Olivia as it slanted its first golden rays across the bed. She opened her eyes with a vague awareness of the man beside her, conscious of the weight of his arm over her body. For a moment, she was too deliciously drowsy to remember—and then, remembering, she was filled with sudden dismay.

As she moved to leave the bed with its heady reminder of shared passion, his arm curved and tightened to draw her back into the warmth of his strong body, proving that he was also awake.

Olivia resisted. 'It's morning,' she told him, rousing him fully. 'I ought not to be here!'

Morgan sighed and rolled over to look at the digital clock beside the bed. Reassured, he turned back to Olivia, oddly reluctant to begin a new day that might threaten their new relationship. He reached for her, smiling. 'I'll have you back at the villa in time for breakfast,' he promised. 'Kiss me . . .'

Olivia evaded him. 'If I hadn't kissed you last night I'd have woken up in my own bed this morning,' she said firmly, without regret. But something flickered in the dark eyes and she hastily bent her head to kiss him, very fleeting. 'I'm not saying that I'm sorry because I'm not! But Celeste will be furious if she finds out!'

There was a little flutter of apprehension about her heart as she sat beside him in the distinctive car as he drove through the village and along the coast road to the large, white-painted Villa Paradis. She was sure that her cousin would be awake and angry, demanding to know why she had been left all night, demanding to know where Olivia had been. Celeste was not easily deceived and Olivia was convinced that the delight she had discovered in Morgan's exciting embrace must be written all over her for everyone to read.

Morgan glanced at her small and slightly anxious face and felt a little wrenching of tenderness that surprised him. He took a hand from the wheel and laid it over her fingers, clasped tightly together in her lap.

'Do you care so much for your cousin's good opinion?' he asked gently.

'I care for her state of mind,' Olivia said bluntly. 'You know how much she likes you, Morgan. It's what you wanted, isn't it? You've been working at it for days!' She tried to keep all hint of reproach or resentment from her voice.

'Applied psychology,' he drawled easily, carelessly.

'And if it succeeds?' Olivia was slightly tense. 'If she falls in love with you—what then?' The concern for her cousin was genuine. It was quite incidental that she was also concerned for the future of her own feeling for this man, she told herself.

Morgan shrugged, laughed. 'Who knows? Maybe I'll fall in love with her,' he returned, teasing her, a smile in the depths of his eyes.

He expected her to laugh and pummel him in mock fury. For he thought it must be obvious that the warm generosity of her giving had dispelled that vague and always half-hearted inclination to fall in love with her beautiful cousin.

Olivia didn't laugh. She didn't even see the dancing mischief in his dark eyes. She thought the words were a warning that she shouldn't be foolish enough to become emotionally involved with him. She felt thankful that he didn't seem to realise that it was much too late.

She knew that he cared for Celeste. She thought of the many small attentions to her cousin of recent days. She thought of the way he had contrived to win Celeste's liking and trust and affection in a very short time. She thought of the way he looked and smiled and spoke whenever he was with Celeste—like a potential lover rather than her doctor, however caring and conscientious! And she thought of the way that he had kissed her sleeping cousin when he held her against his heart.

It was impossible to doubt that he was falling in love whether he knew it yet or not, Olivia decided heavily, facing facts with her usual candour and courage—and remembering with a slight pang that not once had he spoken of loving, for all the passionate ardour and caressing endearments of his lovemaking.

He had made love to her, but only a fool would believe that it meant anything, she told herself firmly. He was a sensual man, a rake and an opportunist, and hadn't she virtually thrown herself at his head? They had both been swept by a tidal wave of desire and her only regret was that she loved him. For it would have been better if she could have walked away with a light heart and dismissed their encounter as easily as he undoubtedly would . . .

'I think you're halfway there already,' she said as lightly as she could.

Morgan raised an amused eyebrow, assuming that she was teasing in her turn. 'Am I?'

He didn't mean to be drawn, Olivia realised. Or he was too kind to admit to a woman who had spent the night in his arms that he cared for her cousin. Her remark had probably been too probing, inviting the rebuff that he was too courteous to give. Instead, he was evasive.

'Perhaps you fall in love with all your patients?' she suggested brightly.

'Only the beautiful ones,' he protested, eyes dancing.

This time she recognised the teasing. 'Oh, of course,' she said, laughing.

He smiled at her, very warm. 'I have been known to fall in love with a beautiful nurse,' he said with a glimmer of mischief.

Olivia didn't dare to hope that the light words held any hint of promise for the future. 'When you were at Kit's, I expect,' she said impulsively. Thinking that he tensed slightly at the words, and remembering his sensitivity about the past, she swiftly wished them unsaid. But it was too late.

He was silent for a moment, manoeuvring a tricky corner. Then he said, cool and deliberate: 'She *was* very beautiful.'

Olivia bit her lip. She longed to know more about the vague mystery that shadowed those days and wished she could remember the elusive details of a scandal that had certainly attached to his name.

'I didn't mean to probe . . .'

'Women always need to know about their predecessors, don't they? But it's a long time ago, you know—and there've been a lot of women since Denise,' he told her bluntly. 'At the time, she was important. Now, she isn't—and I've learned that marriage and medicine just don't mix.'

Olivia glanced at him in surprise. 'I didn't know that you were married!'

'Oh, I wasn't—fortunately. The whole thing blew up in my face just in time,' he said carelessly.

He spoke as though she knew all about it and that was frustrating. Olivia longed to ask questions and felt that she couldn't do so for fear of exposing old wounds to new hurt.

'I'm sorry,' she said quietly, meaning it.

His expression softened. She was very sweet, very warm-hearted. It was touching that she sorrowed for his supposed heartache. He wondered if she was forcibly reminded of her own.

She had gone into his arms so readily that he wondered if she had been so hurt by one man that she was hungry for the comfort to be found in the embrace of another man without giving much thought to the consequences. He suddenly felt a stirring of anger, a sudden dislike of the thought that she might have turned to him on the rebound from the unknown ex-fiancé that she probably still loved. He had no wish to be a substitute lover!

As the Villa Paradis came in sight, Olivia put a hand on his arm. 'Could you stop here? I'll walk the rest of the way along the beach and it will seem that I've just been for a stroll before breakfast. No one will be surprised at that. I really don't want anyone to see me arriving at this hour in your company!'

Morgan nodded, understanding. He brought the car swiftly to a halt. 'We don't wish to arouse suspicion and invite gossip,' he agreed. 'You know how discreet a doctor has to be.' He reached for her hand. 'Thank you for helping me out in the theatre. I'd like to think that you will join us at the clinic eventually. We need nurses like you and you've a natural gift for theatre work. I'm very impressed!'

She had a gift for endearing herself, too, he thought ruefully—but he did not say so. If she was still in love with the man who had let her down then he must not rush into loving her!

'The credit belongs to Kit's,' Olivia said carefully. 'I'm just glad that I was useful.'

'More than useful! That little boy probably owes his life to your prompt response to a cry for help.' She shook her head, demurring. He smiled and suddenly took her small face between both hands and touched her lips with his own in a brief but very tender kiss. 'Lovely Olivia, thank you—for everything,' he said gently.

Her heart crumpled. For that kiss and the soft words seemed to convey a kind of finality and no promise at all for the future.

Perhaps they would never again come together like

destined lovers playing a part in life's vast and mysterious scenario—and maybe it was just as well, Olivia thought heavily.

She clung desperately to her pride, forcing herself to smile and touch his cheek in the lightest of caresses. She knew that she must behave as though it didn't tear her to shreds to realise how unimportant she was in his life. She longed to put her arms about him and admit how much she loved and needed him, how much she ached for some small reassurance for the future.

Instead, she wished him a careless '*au 'voir*' and got out of the car. As it drove away, she looked after it with a sinking heart, feeling that lovers had turned back into virtual strangers with that parting kiss.

She wondered if she could ever meet him again without recalling the magic in his kiss and the wonder in his embrace, without aching to lie in his arms once more. She had known the power and the glory of passion between man and woman and it had been enriched for her by the knowledge that she loved him with all her heart.

For him, it had been one more casual and uncaring encounter with a sexually desirable woman . . .

CHAPTER SEVEN

JEAN-PAUL moved swiftly to intercept her as she walked along the beach, hailing her with an easy friendliness and lightness of manner that didn't betray the shock to his heart.

For he had heard and seen the doctor's familiar car and drawn his own conclusions from the fact that it had stopped some distance away from the Villa Paradis.

He doubted that even an emergency operation and possible complications could have consumed all the hours of the night and there was the bloom of a radiance that he recognised in her enchantingly pretty face as she turned at his call. He knew of the doctor's sensuality and success with women. He was dismayed and disappointed that Olivia seemed to be yet another of the man's many conquests.

'How is *le petit*?' he asked with a genuine interest and concern.

Olivia paused to talk. While she had showered and dressed, Morgan had made a brief visit to the intensive care unit to check on the progress of his young patient. He had returned with the news that the boy was making a good recovery and that the prognosis was excellent. So she was able to pass on that information to Jean-Paul, hoping that she didn't sound too conscious or colour up too obviously as she mentioned the doctor's name.

'*Bon!* But you must be very tired, *chérie*,' he said gently.

She smiled at him warmly, touched by his affection. 'Just a little. Long operations are always a strain for theatre staff.'

'Today, I shall amuse Madame so that you may rest,' he offered.

'Thank you,' she said gratefully. 'But you mustn't neglect your work, Jean-Paul.'

He shrugged. '*N'importe*. I have no desire to work.'

The words were light and the tone careless but Olivia caught just a hint of his disappointment and suddenly realised that she had no secrets from the perceptive young musician. She hoped with all her heart that it would not be equally obvious to Celeste that she had fallen headlong in love with Morgan Beauclerc and spent much of the night in his ardent embrace.

She looked into steady blue eyes that didn't seem to condemn the behaviour that had disappointed his own hopes where she was concerned. She realised on a surge of warm liking that Jean-Paul understood and accepted the situation. She was thankful that she hadn't been too encouraging during the recent days in his company. Jean-Paul was fond of her, she knew—just as she was fond of him. But at least she needn't have his hurt on her conscience, she thought with relief.

They had reached the low gate in the terrace wall and he opened it for her with a flourish. Olivia hesitated. Then, on an impulse, she put an arm about his neck and kissed his cheek. 'I'm sorry,' she said quietly.

He smiled ruefully. 'So am I, *chérie*. If the telephone had not been invented . . . !' He sighed and spread his hands in a very Gallic gesture. '*C'est la vie!* Win some, lose some!' He was suddenly very serious, very tense, as he looked down at her. He raised a hand to the cheek that she had kissed and said, very low: 'I could have loved you, Olivia.' Then he turned and walked away quickly without a backward glance.

'Livvy!' Celeste came out to the terrace in a flowing negligee of apricot silk, flushed with anger and lovelier than ever. 'Where *have* you been! Such a garbled story that Marthe brought in with my tray this morning! What is it all about? And your bed hasn't been slept in!' She looked after the stocky, bronzed figure of the retreating Jean-Paul and her eyes narrowed sharply. 'Oh, Livvy, you fool!' she exclaimed, more in sorrow than anger. 'He's just a boy playing at love and you don't want to be hurt again, surely!'

Olivia opened her mouth to protest at her cousin's mistake, to deny that she had taken Jean-Paul as a lover—and then shut it again.

Better for Celeste to believe that than to be told the truth, perhaps, having regard to her liking for a man who seemed to encourage it for reasons of his own. Marthe knew that she had left last night with Jean-Paul and now Celeste believed that he had brought her back to the villa that morning. An obvious if entirely false conclusion could be drawn from those two facts.

Carefully, Olivia explained about the call from the clinic and the operation at which she had assisted Morgan Beauclerc, allowing her cousin to assume that Jean-Paul had waited for her and then swept her off to his villa for what remained of the night. No lies were actually told, she comforted herself. She had merely omitted much of the truth—and Celeste was much too impatient to listen, anyway.

'I suppose you had to help out, in the circumstances,'

she said, rather grudgingly and obviously annoyed. 'But you're *my* nurse, Livvy. I brought you here to look after me! What if something had happened to me while you were concerning yourself with a sick child and then with your little-boy lover?'

Olivia winced at the selfishness and the scorn of the words. But she did her best to make allowances, reminding herself that Celeste had been ill and was not yet herself. Such a spiteful, jealous reaction was not at all in character, she knew. In normal circumstances, Celeste would be delighted if she could believe that Olivia had swiftly found such consolation in another man's arms after the humiliating experience of losing Keith to someone else.

She had believed that Celeste rather liked Jean-Paul and so she was surprised by that very contemptuous dismissal. Perhaps Celeste liked him too much to see him wasted on another woman, Olivia thought shrewdly, knowing that it was just how her cousin would regard any man's interest in someone other than herself just now. She desperately needed the constant assurance that she was beautiful and desirable and sought-after by every man in her life. Olivia felt that it was most important that Celeste shouldn't learn the truth and turn against Morgan just when she was making such steady progress to please him.

'Darling, I'm sorry,' she said lightly, thinking wryly that the words seemed to be forever on her lips. 'But you must allow me to have some life of my own, you know.' Unconsciously, she was quoting Morgan's words. 'You didn't need me last night . . .'

Celeste broke in abruptly: 'How do you know? And do you care? I must say I'm surprised at your behaviour—and disappointed, too! I know you've had a bad time lately. So have I! But I'm not leaping into bed with men I hardly know as a result!'

Olivia's face flamed, but she held on to her temper. She didn't want to believe that she had only fallen in love on the rebound from Keith or, worse, been swept off her feet and into bed by the charm of one man because of her disappointment in another.

At the same time, she was level-headed and fair-minded enough to admit that either could be the truth. It was probably much too soon to be so sure that she loved Morgan with all her heart and for ever.

'Which probably proves that you're a much nicer person than I am,' she said lightly. 'I'm sorry that you're so upset. But I couldn't refuse to help out in an emergency—and as for the rest . . .' She shrugged, smiled. 'I expect I'm too impulsive.'

'Well, I just hope that you don't have cause to regret it. You're such an innocent,' Celeste said impatiently. 'You allow men to *use* you!'

Olivia wondered with a little shock of surprise at the words if they were true. Had Keith only used her as a convenient girl-friend to show off to his friends and listen to his aims and ambitions and protect him from the amorous pursuit of other girls while he got on with his medical studies? Would Jean-Paul have only used her to satisfy a passing physical need if she had been willing to let him make love to her? And had Morgan only used her because she had been so obviously eager and willing to melt into his arms?

Olivia was much too proud to believe any of it. But Celeste's tiny barbs had a way of sticking in the mind and heart and she found herself recalling that impatient accusation at odd moments throughout the rest of the day.

True to his word, Jean-Paul arrived later, more formally dressed than usual in a light-weight tan suit with matching shirt and tie, driving up in his low-slung sports car instead of walking across the beach and climbing over the wall in his customary fashion.

He seemed older, more self-assured and very handsome in the formal clothes. Olivia thought dryly that he could scarcely be dismissed as a 'little-boy lover' by a scornful Celeste at the present moment. He looked every inch a handsome and successful man. She was prepared to admit that there were occasions when he did seem very young and so light of heart that it was easy to forget the fact that he was a clever and highly-acclaimed composer in his middle twenties.

He had such a boyish, engaging smile, she thought as she went to meet him. 'How nice you look!' she said impulsively, quite forgetting to be constrained by the memory of their last meeting and the thought of the interpretation that her cousin had put on the brief encounter.

He smiled and carried her hand to his lips. 'But you are speaking my lines, *chérie*,' he chided, eyes twinkling.

Olivia laughed, as he had intended. Her heart lifted at the evidence that nothing had changed, after all. He was still her dear, good friend. A sudden thought struck her. 'Are you going away?'

'Not yet. I have come to take Madame out for a drive and some luncheon. Do you approve?'

She almost fell on his neck with gratitude. 'Oh, Jean-Paul! It's just what she needs. She is very cross this morning,' she said with feeling. Then she remembered why Celeste was so cross and her smile faded. She said abruptly: 'I hope you won't be cross, too. She thinks I was with you last night!'

There was the merest pause before he said calmly: 'I won't betray you.' He touched her cheek in a little caress.

Celeste had just put down the telephone after a long conversation with her agent. She should have been heartened to learn that Victor had already lined up several offers of work for the autumn when it was hoped that she would be well enough to return to the theatre. Instead, she was downcast because Victor had nothing to tell with regard to Tom. Apparently, he was away. He had not been seen in any of his usual haunts or by any of his town friends and Celeste didn't care for the implication that he was much too busy with the new woman in his life to have time for friends or frolics.

She almost turned a petulant shoulder to Jean-Paul as he emerged from the house with Olivia in his wake.

They both observed the slight shadow in the lovely violet eyes, the droop of her perfect mouth. Jean-Paul pretended not to notice the slight coolness in her manner as he moved forward to greet her, to take both her slender hands and smile at her with warmth and very genuine admiration.

'*Madame est si belle . . .!*'

Celeste smiled, withdrew her hands from that warm clasp. 'Thank you . . .' She didn't mean to humour him this morning by airing her excellent French. She was not at all pleased with him. Her smile was almost frosty. But her eyes widened fractionally as she took in his debonair elegance.

Olivia knew that her cousin was suddenly impressed.

Until that moment, Celeste had regarded Jean-Paul as little more than a likeable, amusing clown who relieved some of the boredom of the enforced stay in the South of France. Suddenly, she was seeing him in a different light. Suddenly he was an attractive man who had apparently seduced her cousin with ease and might be a possible conquest for herself.

'This seems to be a formal call,' she said with obvious curiosity.

'I am *en route* for Nice,' he explained.

A flicker of disappointment touched the beautiful eyes. 'You are going away?' she asked, unconsciously echoing Olivia's own words and with exactly the same nuance of regret.

'But no, *Madame.* I go only to meet some friends for luncheon. Perhaps it would amuse you to accompany me? I think you are a little bored with the beach, *n'est ce pas*?' His smile and tone were gently persuasive.

Celeste hesitated, glancing at Olivia for her reaction to that unexpected invitation. 'Well, I don't know . . .'

Olivia said firmly: 'It will be too much for you, I'm afraid. You know how quickly you tire!' There wasn't the slightest hint of approval or encouragement in her tone.

Predictably, her cousin promptly chose to accept the invitation. 'I'm sure that Jean-Paul will take excellent care of me,' she said lightly, bestowing her golden smile on him. 'I'm not an invalid or an old lady, Livvy. In fact, I'm feeling very well—and Jean-Paul is right. I *am* bored!'

'But it's so hot today,' Olivia protested for good measure.

'You simply aren't used to the Mediterranean climate,' Celeste said airily. 'It suits me very well and you know that I never wilt in the heat.'

'Well, I don't think I'd care to be far from the beach on a day like this,' Olivia said stoutly.

'Then it's just as well that you are not invited,' Celeste retorted brightly and with obvious satisfaction, sweeping away to change her clothes.

Applied psychology indeed, Olivia thought dryly, thankful to see the back of her demanding and petulant cousin for a few hours. She waved them off, thinking that they made a very handsome couple. Celeste looked particularly lovely in a floral silk suit and matching picture hat and cool, thin-strapped, high-heeled sandals, cheeks flushed and eyes sparkling with the excitement of going off to spend a few hours with an attractive man.

Olivia was very grateful to Jean-Paul for keeping his promise. She had tried to tell him so while he waited for Celeste to dress for the trip to Nice. He had merely smiled and changed the subject. Olivia wondered if he would ever again mention the warmth of an affection that might have blossomed into love.

He liked and admired her and he had briefly desired her, she knew. But it seemed that he accepted that she thought of him as friend rather than lover. Perhaps it hadn't hurt too much to discover that she thought of Morgan Beauclerc as lover rather than friend . . .

The afternoon seemed long and lonely and Olivia couldn't help thinking that it might have been better spent with the attractive and exciting doctor than in lazing in the sunshine and writing a few letters to friends.

He did not mean to call to see his patient that day. She wondered if he was busy at the clinic or if he was taking time off from the demands of being a doctor.

Drowsing on a lounger on the terrace, it was impossible not to be thinking of him constantly, missing him and aching for him. Once, she reached out her hand to the telephone on the impulse to call him—and then checked. Somehow it just wasn't possible for her to do so. Perhaps she was old-fashioned, just as she had told him, but she felt that she couldn't run after a man who might only regard her as a casual conquest.

She thought with longing of his ardent and much too experienced lovemaking. She thought of the crispness of his dark hair to her touch, the slight and very human roughness of his beard in the early morning, the muscular strength of his lean frame and the surprising sensitivity of those surgeon's hands on her body. She thought of his kiss, his touch, his nearness, and knew that she loved him.

New to the wonderful world of sexual delight, its echo still quivering in the deepest part of her being, Olivia's body throbbed with longing for his embrace. New to the demanding and disturbing world of loving, her heart swelled and sorrowed because it was only too likely that he was much too busy or much too disinterested to give her a thought on that sunny afternoon. Yet they might have been together.

She realised for the first time that loving could be a curse rather than a blessing when it was one-sided. She felt an even greater sympathy for her unhappy cousin who had married the man she loved and then lost him to another woman. Olivia had very little to remember. But she knew that she would never forget, never cease to love, never find real happiness with any other man.

So what must Celeste feel after two years of loving and

living with Tom Knight? Of course she was desperately unhappy, ill and depressed and bitter, unable to accept or to make a new life for herself! A woman could face the death of the man she loved with courage. His heartless desertion of her for another woman could be a mortal blow.

Of course the doctors couldn't cure Celeste's anxiety and apathy, root of her illness! She was heartsick. She had been deeply humiliated. She felt that she no longer had anything to live for . . . not even the career that had once mattered so much to her.

'. . . *love is of man's life a thing apart, 'tis woman's whole existence* . . .'

Byron's famous words rose in Olivia's mind with a new awareness of their truth. For two years, Celeste had allowed her life to revolve around Tom. Without that axis, the security of his affection and support even if he denied her his love, she was totally lost.

Olivia knew that Morgan recognised that fact. But she doubted if even his cleverness combined with an undeniable physical magnetism could arouse more than a flicker of response in a woman who loved as deeply as Celeste loved her husband.

She might be an instinctive flirt who enjoyed exercising the power of her beauty and desirability over almost every man she met, encouraging admiration and attention in very feminine fashion, needing to be loved and wanted. But there was only one man that she truly wanted with all her heart—and that heart was slowly breaking because Tom did not want her at all.

She might have returned hate with hate, the other side of the doubtful coin called love. But she could not cope with the grey wall of indifference, so alien to her own passionate nature that knew only black and white, love and hate.

If only it was possible to wave a magic wand and bring Tom back, loving and repentant, Olivia thought heavily, having discovered that being nurse cum companion to someone as complex as an ill and unhappy Celeste was more demanding than she had expected. But magic wands were few and far between in life—and if she had one, she might be more tempted to use it to bring about her own happiness with Morgan, much as she cared about her cousin!

At the sound of the car in the late afternoon, Olivia hurried out with warmly affectionate concern for the well-being of her patient, knowing that she would obstinately refuse to admit that the day with Jean-Paul had exhausted her small reserve of strength.

Celeste was bubbling. She had enjoyed the drive—and the shops, she announced with a faint air of defiance, presenting Olivia with a flask of perfume, a silk scarf and a pretty brooch with her usual extravagant generosity.

Lunch had been great fun, she declared, sparkling. Jean-Paul's friend had turned out to be a well-known French singer who was interested in recording some of his songs. His English wife was an actress who had once appeared in a play with Celeste and they had been delighted to meet again. They had talked a great deal of amusing 'shop' while the two men talked music.

Jean-Paul was a dear, a delightful companion, so kind and thoughtful and understanding, she enthused. He was very attractive, too, she added, with a flirtatious and very mischievous glance for the rather silent man by her side.

They would have tea on the terrace, she decided airily, and went off to her room with a swirl of skirts and a drift of expensive perfume to change into something cool and comfortable.

Olivia smiled at Jean-Paul and linked her hand in his arm, drawing him out to the terrace. 'Thank you,' she said warmly. 'It's good to see her looking so happy.' She knew it wouldn't last. Celeste was so volatile, up in the clouds one moment and in the pit of absolute despair the next. But she was grateful to Jean-Paul for giving her a good day.

He smiled wryly. 'She has heard something to please her, *chérie.* Now she is walking on air. The affair of her husband is over. Pamela talked of nothing else. She has a good heart but she is not tactful.'

Olivia's heart quickened with new hope for Celeste's happiness—and then plummeted as she realised what her cousin evidently did not and what Jean-Paul had also realised with his swift and sensitive perception.

If Tom's affair with another woman had ended, he had not hurried back to his unhappy wife as a result! He had never loved Celeste at all, Olivia believed. He obviously did not want her now. It would be even worse for Celeste to discover that it was not a rival that kept him from her side but true indifference, she thought with sudden dread.

'How does she know . . . this Pamela?' she asked quickly. 'Celeste was talking to her agent only this morning and he said nothing about it.'

'Pamela has been in Paris with some friends. She knows him well from the days before she married Claude. They met by chance, had a drink together, talked. Perhaps he needed a confidante. But he didn't speak of Celeste and Pamela didn't know that she was also in France. She is a romantic. Now . . .' His grimace was expressive.

Olivia leaned forward, apprehensive. 'Celeste thinks he must be looking for her, I suppose?'

He nodded. 'It is evident, *n'est ce pas*?'

'Wishful thinking!'

'*Pardon . . . ?*'

'Oh—fantasy!' Olivia's tone was rueful.

'You do not think it is possible?'

'No, I don't. Why Paris? She was in London until recently and she made no secret of her plans to come here to convalesce. She told the world in the hope that Tom would hear of it, in fact! She's such an optimist. I don't know what he's doing in France, but I don't think he has the slightest interest in his wife,' she said, rather bitterly.

'She is very much in love,' he said with understanding.

Olivia nodded. 'Yes.'

The telephone tinkled as someone lifted the receiver of one of the many extensions in the house. Olivia and Jean-Paul exchanged glances.

'She's ringing every hotel in Paris to find him,' Olivia said heavily, knowing her cousin and dreading the outcome. 'And if she does manage to trace him, he'll refuse to talk to her.' She sighed. 'She's very near a complete breakdown, mental and physical. I'm so afraid for her . . .'

Jean-Paul reached for her hand and pressed it gently, silent. She sensed his compassion, the concern of a caring and kindly man. She wondered wryly why women like herself and her cousin fell in love with rakes and rogues when there were reliable and responsible men like Jean-Paul in the world—and knew that Jean-Paul, dear though he might always be, could never touch her heart or stir her senses with the all-important magic of loving.

For her, there was only Morgan.

Just as, for Celeste, there was only Tom . . .

CHAPTER EIGHT

THAT evening, Olivia and Jean-Paul dined on the terrace with the superb splendour of a Mediterranean sunset for backcloth and the gentle boom of the waves against the shore for orchestra. It was a romantic setting and he was an attractive and attentive man. She was much too tense to appreciate any of it.

A suddenly crumpled Celeste had opted to eat dinner off a tray in her room, pleading that she was tired. Olivia doubted if her cousin would eat more than a morsel of Marthe's culinary efforts, designed to tempt the most capricious appetite. No mention had been made of the obviously abortive telephone calls to Paris. Olivia knew that the euphoria of the day's excitement had suddenly evaporated, leaving Celeste plunged into a too-familiar despair.

She was vaguely uneasy throughout the meal. Jean-Paul, understanding, kept up a steady flow of easy, undemanding conversation that scarcely required answer from someone whose mind was obviously elsewhere for most of the time. He had not refused the invitation to dine at the villa, knowing that she needed the soothing reassurance of his company if nothing else—and he was an optimist. If she could give herself to one man, then why not another—if mood and moment was right? Both were wrong at the present time, but there was no reason why he shouldn't pave the way a little.

Suddenly Olivia put down her glass of wine and rose from the table with a murmur of apology and hurried to her cousin's room. A trained nurse developed a kind of sixth sense for knowing when something was wrong with her patient.

She found Celeste sitting on the edge of her bed in flimsy underthings, all colour drained from her lovely face, eyes wide and terror-stricken and a hand clutched to her heart.

'Oh, Livvy . . . thank God!' she gasped as Olivia swiftly crossed to her side. 'Oh, Livvy, I'm so frightened! I'm going to die! I know I'm going to die!'

She was trembling from head to toe in quite uncontrollable panic, beads of sweat on her forehead and a clammy coldness of the hands that clutched at Olivia in alarm and apprehension. Tense and anxious, she was fighting waves of faintness that she regarded as the certain harbinger of death, untimely and dreaded.

Olivia had coped with similar attacks but they had been lessening, happening at longer intervals. Now she dealt with this one with her usual brisk efficiency that discounted unnecessary sympathy while reassuring her cousin. Celeste was feeling quite sorry enough for herself and it wasn't kindness to encourage her in self-pity, she knew. At the same time, it was essential to convince her that she was a very long way from dying.

The attacks were alarming while they lasted but unfounded on anything but an anxiety that stemmed from unhappiness and a stubborn refusal to face facts. Olivia firmly believed that her cousin was suffering from a psychogenic illness, but it wasn't easy to convince someone as vulnerable as Celeste that her frightening symptoms were all in the mind, she thought wryly.

Celeste had an obsessive belief that she would never see her husband again, quite literally. Her subconscious mind refused to accept that it might be the result of indifference on his part and translated it into the conviction that she was destined to die in the near future. And, obligingly, her subconscious mind provided the necessary symptoms to back up a quite baseless dread.

It was a form of hysteria that attacked when she was over-tired or over-stimulated or particularly depressed. Olivia knew that Morgan would feel that she had failed to take proper care of her patient. His careful instructions had been ignored—and this was the result.

It was a much milder attack than previous ones, quite short-lived, but it was an unwelcome setback when Celeste had been making such good progress. Olivia gave her a sedative and gradually she quietened, ceased to shake, breathed more easily and was no longer afraid of slipping into unconsciousness if she once relaxed her guard.

But she was far from tranquil and she refused to be left alone. She would not go to bed. She was afraid to sleep. She wanted to talk about Tom, wanted to know if Olivia thought it could be true that he was no longer living with Anna, wanted confirmation of her own wild hope that he would arrive at the villa within the next few days.

Olivia was evasive, reluctant to bolster the hopes and equally reluctant to shatter them. She said as little as possible in reply, trying to turn her cousin's thoughts in a different direction, trying to coax her to relax and settle down to sleep.

Celeste became petulant. 'Oh, you aren't interested! You don't care! You're as selfish as everyone else, thinking about your own affairs. You want me tucked up safely in bed so you can get back to being alone with Jean-Paul, I suppose!'

'Well, of course,' Olivia said lightly, smiling, humouring her as she usually did. 'But if you insist on playing gooseberry . . .' She reached for her cousin's robe and held it out to her.

Celeste slipped her arms into the loose, flowing sleeves, slightly mollified. 'Do you like him so much?' she asked curiously. 'You're wasting your time, you know. He's very sweet, but Pamela says that he's had dozens of women and I don't suppose that you're anything special. Do yourself a favour and don't get too involved, Livvy.'

Olivia felt that she could safely promise that much but she merely slipped mules on to her cousin's feet and straightened.

Jean-Paul turned as the two women entered the sitting-room, sufficiently at home in the villa to have quietly finished his dinner and poured himself a drink.

He was very concerned, feeling he was to blame for Celeste's exhaustion and thankful that she was already feeling well enough to leave her room for the evening.

He set himself to be attentive and gradually the colour returned to her face and she seemed to relax. He stayed for some time because Celeste clung to him as though she no longer trusted Olivia. He was very kind, very gentle and very patient.

When he finally went away, Olivia had only a few moments alone with him before her cousin called her back to the sitting-room.

'You're a good friend, Jean-Paul,' she told him warmly. 'But I can't help feeling that we are making too much use of you!' Her smile was rueful.

He took both her hands and held them very tightly, smiling into her troubled eyes. 'I do it for you, Olivia,' he said softly, meaning it.

'For so little reward!' she exclaimed with her impulsive candour. And, on another impulse, she leaned against him and kissed him on the lips. 'Thank you, anyway!'

'Sufficient reward!' he said promptly, eyes dancing.

Olivia shook her head, laughing. 'I doubt it!'

Jean-Paul put an arm about her slight waist and drew her close in sudden, unmistakable longing. 'Then kiss me again, *chérie* . . .'

She did so, very lightly, and heard the soft, wry sigh that escaped him.

She was very fond of Jean-Paul. He was so reliable and kind and warm-hearted. He seemed to have a sensitive understanding of a woman's need to inspire much more than sexual hunger in a man. But she knew she could never love him. The heart had its own reasons for an emotion that had nothing to do with what was wise or sensible or likely to end in lasting happiness.

Enfolding her, Jean-Paul held her against him for a moment, lips pressed to her hair. Olivia felt him tremble and she was suddenly saddened by the depth of his desire and her own lack of response. She thought how her body quickened for the merest touch of Morgan's hand. She recalled the long association with Keith and her seeming frigidity. For her, love and sexual longing were apparently synonymous. The chemistry was right where Morgan was concerned. It could never be anything but totally wrong with a man she did not love.

Jean-Paul said abruptly: 'I shall be away for a few days, Olivia. I'll let you know when I am back.'

Olivia drew away, surprised and slightly dismayed. She had come to rely on him, she realised. She wondered if it was a sudden decision or if he had not found the right opportunity to speak of his plans earlier in the evening.

'We shall miss you,' she said, lightly but sincere. 'I'm afraid we are spoiled by seeing so much of you. I'm sure you've neglected all your other friends—*and* your work.'

'Not my work. That has found a new source of inspiration,' he told her, smiling.

It was flattery but she believed it to be meant and she was moved. She smiled at him with warm affection.

Celeste called, peremptory, and Jean-Paul pressed a kiss into the palm of Olivia's hand and went away. She wondered as she hurried to her cousin when she would see him again . . .

All that night, Celeste veered between moods. At one moment, she was sure that Tom had come to France in search of her and that she would see him very soon, too excited to sleep and refusing to be left and firmly rejecting the pills that Olivia wished her to take, talking eagerly and wildly about the future.

The next moment, she was utterly downcast and clinging to Olivia in floods of tears as the only person who really cared anything for her, declaring that everyone else kept Tom away from her with a succession of lies.

Then defiant, angry, insisting that she no longer loved Tom anyway and didn't want to see him and would send him away if he came to the villa, accusing Olivia of forcing sleeping tablets on her so that she could be free to spend another night in Jean-Paul's waiting arms.

Olivia calmed and comforted throughout the long and

difficult night, ignoring insults and flattery alike, suppressing a very natural inclination to slap her cousin at times and reminding herself firmly that Celeste was patient as much as relative who felt that the family tie allowed her to say and do whatever she pleased.

Celeste was exhausted by morning and Olivia was thankful when her patient slipped into a fretful, restless doze. She took the offered opportunity for a quick shower and a change of clothes and then sat down gratefully to hot coffee and Marthe's delicious croissants.

She was watching for Morgan's car long before it turned into the drive and drew up outside the house. Olivia went out to meet him with mingled shyness and apprehension, a hint of colour in her small face and eyes bright from lack of sleep and the strain of coping with her difficult cousin.

Morgan looked at her keenly. 'You look tired,' he said without preliminary.

It was foolish to be disappointed because there was nothing of the lover in that greeting or in his manner. He was very formal, a doctor calling on his patient. The night in his arms might never have been, Olivia thought with a catch of dismay.

'Celeste had a bad night,' she said carefully. She explained the attack and its probable cause and continued effect.

Morgan listened, frowning. 'And you encouraged her to go to Nice? Against my explicit instructions?'

Olivia's heart sank at that disapproving tone although she had expected it and knew that his annoyance was fully justified. 'Yes, I did,' she admitted candidly.

Morgan reached to take his case from the car. 'May I

ask why?' He tried to keep a certain disappointment from his voice. He had thought her so reliable, so caring. It was not like a Kit's nurse to flout a doctor's wishes for his patient.

Olivia hesitated. Then she said quietly: 'She was in a particularly difficult mood yesterday morning. I thought it might do us both good to be away from each other for a while.'

Morgan's eyes narrowed abruptly. He was doing his best not to recall the delight of this woman in his arms, but the remembered perfume of her hair and her soft voice and the delicate prettiness was playing havoc with his resolution.

She had been constantly in his thoughts during the past twenty-four hours and that was disturbing for a man who had always found it easy to dismiss a woman from mind when he didn't wish to think about her. Now, he was consumed with the sudden longing to touch her, to kiss her, to hold her in his arms—and that was even more disturbing. For in the past, he had always been able to separate the professional from the personal in his life.

'Repercussions?' he asked abruptly.

He hadn't meant to refer to their intimacy at such an inappropriate moment. But he couldn't ignore the slight hesitation of voice and manner as she spoke of her cousin's frame of mind following that overnight absence from the villa. He had doubted that she would explain it away too easily. But she was a grown woman and she did not have to answer to anyone for her actions.

'There might have been more but Celeste believes that I spent the night with Jean-Paul,' Olivia told him, rather reluctantly. She hadn't meant to mention the utterly unforgettable experience that he seemed intent on forgetting as soon as he could. His brusque tone implied that he had not wished to be reminded of the night they had spent in each other's arms, proving how very little it had meant to him. Her heart swelled with sudden hurt and humiliation.

'Good God!'

Her face flamed. No doubt she was being over-sensitive, but it seemed to her that there was an amused mockery in that immediate reaction to her words. Did he think it so impossible that a woman would prefer someone like Jean-Paul to an experienced sensualist like himself? He was so arrogant, much too sure of himself, Olivia thought angrily, bridling with a defensive indignation on Jean-Paul's behalf and almost wishing that she *had* taken him as her very first lover instead of this man.

'It could have happened,' she said sharply, chin tilting. 'Celeste knows how we feel about each other!'

The words were badly chosen. She had only meant to imply that a great deal of affection existed between herself and Jean-Paul. Morgan immediately supposed that they were in love and that her irritation sprang from a sense of guilt because she had been swept off her feet and into bed by his physical magnetism.

She had come to him as a virgin but now he wondered wryly if that had been merely a matter of timing. On the rebound from a broken engagement, she might have been ready to fall into the arms of any man who took a certain amount of flattering interest in her. And Jean-Paul with his lively manner and engaging charm was a formidable rival with much more time to devote to the amorous pursuit of Olivia than a busy doctor. Perhaps only circumstances, combination of mood and moment, had favoured him.

He discovered a fierce dislike of her association with the other man and her obvious regret for what had happened between them. He didn't immediately recognise it as jealousy.

'Then it seems she had good reason to believe the lie,' he said carefully, cool with the effort to keep all betraying emotion from his tone.

Olivia suspected that he was contemptuous. Very hurt, but realising that she had given him good cause to despise her as a too-easy conquest, she said quickly: 'No one lied! Celeste just leapt to a very natural conclusion, in the circumstances.' She almost added bitterly that if she had to lose her virginity so impulsively and so unexpectedly then it was probably disastrous that she had chosen a rake instead of the warm-hearted Jean-Paul who wouldn't have treated her like a virtual stranger at their next encounter! She bit back the words. 'Should I have told her the truth?' she asked, very dry. 'That would have been more of a setback for her than the trip to Nice, in my opinion. She looks upon you as her property, you know. She certainly doesn't want Jean-Paul!'

He raised an eyebrow. 'Yet she went to Nice with him!'

'Of course. With one stroke, she showed me that she could take him away from me if she wished—and that I'm a gullible fool to believe that any man can be trusted. I should have thought that her motives wouldn't need explaining to someone with your clever grasp of feminine pyschology,' she added sweetly.

Morgan acknowledged the hit with a faint smile. 'It seems that I don't know enough about your cousin. Certainly I thought that she was fond of you.'

'But she is! To her mind, she's protecting my interests. She thinks I'm too trusting and too impulsive,' Olivia said brightly, leading the way into the house. 'And she's quite right!'

Morgan caught the faint barb in her tone, intended for him. He knew enough about women to understand the slight hostility and unmistakable resentment of her attitude to him that morning. She had yielded to an instinct as old as time and regretted it. She was not the first woman to wish that she had kept her head and her virginity and to feel that a man was best kept at arms length for a while. And perhaps that vague mistrust of him, dating from the stories that had circulated about him at Kit's, still lingered.

He was sorry that she was not liking him very much at the moment. But it was not unexpected. In fact, it was a very natural reaction. In normal circumstances, he would have known just how to combat it. But Jean-Paul was threatening the delicate balance of their new relationship and Olivia seemed to be making it very clear that they didn't have any kind of a future, he thought ruefully, rather shaken to realise that she was the one woman who could be of real importance in his life.

There had been so many women. No-one like Olivia with her sweetness and warmth and integrity, her unassuming loveliness and strength of character. She possessed an inexplicable enchantment for him that had been weaving its spell since the first moment of meeting.

He had spent a lot of time at the Villa Paradis that week on the pretext of familiarising himself with an unusual case and certainly fascinated to some extent by the beauty of his patient. But, in reality, he had been drawn by the attractions of a girl who had tried very hard not to show that she found him attractive, too.

The chemistry had sparked an instant and very positive reaction between them at first sight. It had been inevitable that they should become lovers. Morgan had anticipated a light-hearted and very enjoyable and probably short-lived affair like all the others. He hadn't expected to find himself falling in love . . .

He questioned her very closely about Celeste's sudden attack of illness and listened intently as she recounted each classic symptom, nodding from time to time. 'Why didn't you call me?' he asked at the end of the recital.

'It didn't seem to be necessary.' She was slightly on the defensive. 'She's had several of these attacks and I know how to deal with them.'

'I wished to see for myself just how they affect her at the time. Never mind. Perhaps she can be persuaded to spend a few days in the clinic so that I can carry out some necessary tests. How is she at present?'

'Very tired, very volatile.' Olivia opened the door of Celeste's bedroom. 'She's been very anxious to see you. She trusts you to tell her the truth.'

'Then you should have telephoned,' he told her with a slight impatience of tone. 'I might have made this my first call instead of the last.'

Olivia couldn't explain that he might have suspected her of making an excuse to talk to him. So she was silent, smarting slightly from his tone and feeling rebuked.

Celeste stirred, half-smiled, held out her hand in swift, eager greeting as though she regarded him as a lifeline. 'Morgan . . .' she said, very warm, like a woman in love.

He took her hand and bent over her with that very

attractive smile in his dark eyes. Olivia thought he meant to kiss her cousin and her heart shook. 'I'm sorry to hear that you aren't so well today, Mrs Knight,' he said gently, the formality that he still insisted on using sounding like an endearment, so obviously more concerned for her as a man than as her doctor that Olivia's heart contracted.

He had made love to her with the passionate and probably meaningless ardour of a sensual man. Now he spoke and smiled for Celeste with something very special in his voice and manner, she thought bleakly.

Her cousin was so appealing, so vulnerable, that men went down like ninepins before that fragile and delicate beauty. They all fell in love with her, yearned to cherish her, wished to spend their lives as her devoted slave—all except Tom who just didn't give a damn for his lovely wife! No wonder that it was Tom that Celeste insisted on wanting so much that she became ill with frustration and despair!

Celeste told Morgan all about her day with Jean-Paul, challenging him to scold. He didn't. She told him about the wave of illness that had left her feeling wretched and shaken. He was sympathetic and reassuring.

The perfect bedside manner, Olivia thought absently, not really listening as she stood at the foot of the bed. She had unconsciously adopted the traditional pose of the attendant nurse, quite unaware that it was irritating her cousin who disliked the reminder of a certain rapport between doctor and nurse.

Celeste suddenly snapped: 'I do wish you wouldn't *hover*, Livvy! This isn't a hospital ward and you don't have to impress anyone with your air of efficiency! It isn't as though you're such a credit to St Christopher's, after all. You aren't at all reliable!'

Olivia swallowed the instinctive and very angry retort as she met the warm sympathy in Morgan's swift glance. She even managed a smile. 'I'm glad that my badge is all the reference I need,' she said lightly. 'It didn't come with a packet of cornflakes, you know!'

Morgan chuckled. 'No, indeed! Hard-earned, in fact. I can vouch for that! You're in excellent hands, Mrs Knight. I've every confidence in Oliv . . . Miss Paine. Although she shouldn't have allowed you to go on that jaunt to Nice,' he added hastily, suddenly remembering that it wasn't wise to praise one woman to another in this particular instance.

Celeste's lovely eyes held a gleam of satisfaction. Olivia was thankful that her cousin hadn't noticed the slight slip of Morgan's careless tongue. 'Oh, were you cross with Livvy?' she asked sweetly. 'She tried to stop me, you know. I wouldn't listen.'

'Well, you will listen to *me*. Or find yourself another doctor,' he told her, very firm. 'As for Miss Paine, I'm sure she now realises the importance of obeying my instructions.'

A slight colour rose in Olivia's face at the autocratic tone. She felt exactly like a first-year nurse being put firmly in her place by a crusty senior consultant. 'Yes, Doctor,' she said meekly. The suddenly militant sparkle in her grey eyes almost declared '*go to hell, Doctor*'. But she remembered just in time that a Kit's nurse was too well-trained even to entertain such a rebellious thought . . .

CHAPTER NINE

RESPONDING to his masterful manner, Celeste agreed to enter the Beauclerc Clinic that afternoon. She was obviously torn between the pleasing prospect of seeing a great deal of the attractive doctor and the heady hope that Tom would turn up at the villa in search of her. But she finally accepted the idea when Morgan declared that he would drive her to the clinic in his own car.

Olivia wondered dryly if he offered that kind of service to all his patients—or just the beautiful ones. It was becoming increasingly obvious that he was very interested in Celeste. Perhaps he wanted her at the clinic so that he could persuade his brother to take over her case, leaving him free to treat her as a woman instead of his patient.

Olivia knew that his feeling for Celeste went much deeper than the physical attraction that she had excited in him. Like so many men, he was falling deeply in love with her lovely cousin. Unlike those other men, it seemed possible that he might become a necessary part of Celeste's life. She might always love Tom, but a woman often settled for second best and she was rapidly becoming dependent on Morgan for a degree of happiness, it seemed.

He was very attractive and he had charm. He was a mature and sophisticated and sensual man of the world. He had a reputation as a sensitive and caring doctor. Married to him, Celeste would find all the emotional security and stability that she so desperately needed.

And if she married him when the divorce from Tom became final, Olivia would have to walk out of her cousin's life for ever. It was hard enough now to be in the same room with him, loving him, wanting him. As Celeste's husband, it would be unbearable torment.

Now, she longed to be in his arms, to know his kiss and the ecstasy of his lovemaking. Then, she wouldn't even be able to risk the touch of his hand. For she knew instinctively that the bright flame of passion would always burn between them, no matter what he felt for Celeste or any other woman. Something undeniably sparked for the meeting of their eyes in the most casual of glances. Sexually, they ignited each other as though they had always been destined to be lovers.

Loving him, Olivia wanted with all her heart for him to love and need her. She knew without shame that she would take anything at all that he offered, with or without love on his part.

But she couldn't hurl herself at him. She had to be the well-trained nurse who was concerned for the welfare of her patient—and at the same time she had to be the caring cousin who was concerned for the well-being of all the family she had. It left little time or energy for being a woman in love, Olivia thought wryly.

Admitted to the clinic, Celeste immediately began to panic. She didn't need any tests, she said. She didn't want any further investigations. She swung predictably from the conviction that X-ray or blood test, electrocardiogram or electro-encephalograph or scanner, would reveal something that had been previously overlooked to the declaration that it was a waste of everyone's time and her money when there was absolutely nothing wrong with her. It was obvious that she was terrified that an obscure clinic in a French province would come up with an answer that the famous London specialists had failed to provide for all their efforts. If she was dying from some mysterious disease not yet identified, then she didn't want to know it!

'Very well,' Morgan said indifferently, turning to the door. 'I certainly haven't the wish to waste my time or your money, Mrs Knight. I'm quite sure that there isn't anything wrong with you, as it happens. Miss Paine will help you to dress and I'll arrange for a car for you.' He walked out of the room, quietly closing the door.

Celeste wasn't used to such high-handed treatment. Strangely, she didn't seem to resent it. She lay back on the pillows, ethereally fair and very lovely and rather pleased with herself, and smiled at Olivia. 'Damn the man!' she said lightly. 'He thinks I'm just neurotic! I expect he's right, too. I suppose I must agree to his beastly tests just to prove it. Go and tell him that I'll stay!'

Olivia found him in the corridor, just as she had expected. She was surprised that such patently transparent methods should work so well with her very intelligent if temperamental cousin. But Celeste had a sense of humour—even if it had been buried under a mountain of depression in recent weeks.

Morgan stood by a long window, hands deep in the pockets of his white coat, tall and dark and much too attractive—and looking every inch the clever and capable doctor so beloved of romantic novelists, she thought dryly.

He was studying a group of spina bifida children in the garden below, benefiting from the sunshine and the carefully prescribed exercises that were being carried out or supervised by the overalled physiotherapists. The children were the subject of some intensive research into the problem by his dedicated half-brother. Olivia felt that she would like to meet Gerard Beauclerc. He was spoken of with a great deal of warmth and even more respect by staff and patients at the clinic, she had noticed. Morgan obviously considered it a privilege to work with him at the clinic that he had founded.

He turned at Olivia's approach, a glimmer of amusement in the dark eyes. 'Well? Is she staying?'

'Of course.'

He nodded. 'Of course,' he agreed, very dry. His smile deepened. 'I'll do my best to keep her content for a few days, Olivia. You deserve a rest from coping with those moods. Relax and enjoy it. Swim, sunbathe, go sailing with Jean-Paul—and get lots of sleep,' he added, touching the faint smudges of weariness beneath the grey eyes in an almost-caress.

Olivia quivered and was furious with herself for that betraying response to his touch. 'Yes, Doctor,' she said, mock demure, using levity as a mask for her swift resentment at the words.

'And watch those impulses!' he teased, eyes twinkling. *Don't succumb to Jean-Paul's blandishments*, he meant, feeling a very real anxiety on that score and knowing that he didn't have the right to express it.

The beginnings of a blush stole into her face. 'Yes, I will,' she returned, very light. *And particularly where you are concerned*, she added silently, on a surge of pride.

She was hurt by the careless, arbitrary handing-over of her to another man, the unmistakable implication of his instructions. She would need to be very naive not to know that he was dismissing her from his life. Their brief intimacy was not likely to be repeated and she should forget all about him, he was declaring. Jean-Paul was an approved substitute for her interest and her passion! Damn him! How dared he dispose of her emotions in that arrogant fashion! How dared he take her in the heat of desire and then turn away with such careless indifference and not the slightest regard for her feelings! She *would* go sailing with Jean-Paul! She would encourage him at every turn! She would probably leap into bed with him at the first opportunity—and to hell with Morgan Beauclerc! It wouldn't give her the slightest satisfaction, of course. But it would show him that she cared as little for him as he obviously cared for her!

The villa seemed empty and lonely without her cousin. Olivia was not used to having time on her hands. The days had been very full and satisfying when she was working at Kit's and the last weeks with Celeste had taken all her time and energy—and she had been glad of it. She might have fretted for Keith if she hadn't been so concerned for Celeste's health and happiness.

Now, the years of caring for Keith and hoping to marry him seemed very unreal and remote. She had been very young and immature and totally unawakened, she realised. Suddenly, she knew all about loving as it should be—and wished she did not!

Olivia ate dinner in solitary splendour, discovering that she had very little appetite but forcing herself to do justice to Marthe's superb cooking. *She* didn't mean to give way to heaviness of heart and the bleak belief that life held very little for her if she wasn't loved by one particular man, she told herself sternly.

She spent the evening reading and listening to music, missing Jean-Paul who might have been with her if she hadn't been so discouraging. She was sure that he had gone away to get over the disappointment she had dealt him with the indifference that she just couldn't hide and the preference for Morgan that had been equally obvious to him.

She went to bed early and slept without dreaming. She rose early to breakfast on the terrace, feeling refreshed and full of energy if not optimism, wondering how she would fill the day without Celeste to worry about and look after. This was an unexpected holiday that she really didn't want, she thought wryly. It would be much better for her to be too busily occupied to yearn after the attractive and elusive doctor.

The beach was quiet and very beautiful at that hour. The heat shimmered on the golden sand even so early in the morning and the sea sparkled in the bright sunlight. Leafy palm trees provided some shade for the white-painted splendour of the Villa Paradis. It might be Paradise indeed, Olivia thought—with the right person to share it with her.

Later that morning, she walked into the village for flowers and fruit and books to take to Celeste, managing very well despite her limited French and deciding that Jean-Paul would be pleased with her improved accent.

During the short bus ride into the pleasant countryside where the clinic was situated, she continued to think about Jean-Paul and to wonder when he would be coming back. It kept her from thinking of Morgan and hoping that he would be at the clinic when she reached it.

As she walked up the gravel drive towards the recently-built and very impressive main building, Olivia passed the low, green-tiled wing of the original mansion that housed Morgan's flat. Memories came flooding and she wished that she had as much courage as she had love for him. But it would take more confidence than she possessed at present to mount the stone steps and knock on the green-painted door. She had a very clear picture of the flat's interior etched on her mind's eye. She had a very clear picture of Morgan, too, smiling at her with that particular warmth in his dark eyes that had swept her into loving him all in a moment.

The magic and the madness of that night had changed her life completely. She would always love him and she couldn't go back to being a virgin. Their lives were irrevocably linked by that passionate encounter, she felt. A woman never forgot her first sexual experience and if she happened to love the man then he occupied a very special place in her heart and memory until the day she died.

So Morgan must always be important to her. But she couldn't ask anything of him. Loving him gave her no rights and if he chose to behave as though he had nothing to remember where she was concerned then there wasn't a thing she could do about it.

As she neared the main part of the clinic, Morgan came through the swing doors, tall and distinctive in formal grey suit, dark hair neatly brushed, black doctor's bag in hand. Her heart bumped painfully against her ribs and she paused, undecided, in the shadow of some trees. He seemed to be in a hurry, heading for his parked car. He might or might not have noticed her, she felt, hesitating to attract his attention.

Morgan saw a flash of white frock against the dark

background out of the corner of his eye and glanced towards her. He checked and then began to walk towards her, smiling. He was astonished to discover that a heart really could leap with delight. He had always supposed it to be an absurd romantic fiction.

She was slender and pretty in the short summer frock of broderie anglaise cotton, a ribbon bound about her bright curls to keep them from her neck, arms filled with flowers and parcels. But although she smiled at him there was a coolness in the grey eyes. Morgan felt rebuffed. If she was pleased to see him it certainly didn't show, he thought wryly.

'I didn't expect to see you here so early,' he greeted her lightly. 'I meant to call at the villa on my rounds.'

Olivia thought it was a polite fiction. Why should he wish to see her? Hadn't he pushed her towards Jean-Paul with both hands, quite unmistakably? 'How is Celeste today?' she asked brightly. 'I did telephone but she was sleeping.'

'In excellent spirits,' he told her, smile deepening. 'She thrives on plenty of attention, as you know.'

And no doubt you mean to give her just as much as she needs, Olivia thought heavily, struck by a note of tender affection in his deep voice and a certain glow of warmth in his dark eyes. She was very conscious of him, so attractive and so disturbing that it unsteadied her foolish heart. She was determined not to let it show for she was also very conscious of his cool and almost impersonal manner. He had smiled at sight of her, paused to speak to her, but Olivia couldn't feel that there was any real interest in his attitude. It seemed very obvious that her only claim to be noticed by him these days sprang from her kinship to Celeste. Concern for her cousin was all that they had in common, it seemed. Strangers who had briefly become lovers had turned into strangers again.

'The ECG showed no sign of abnormality, just as expected,' Morgan went on. 'She seems to be finally convinced that her heart is in splendid condition and she's much more relaxed as a result.'

'She hasn't believed or trusted any other doctor who told her exactly the same thing,' Olivia said, rather dryly. 'What it is to have charm!' She meant to be flippant. It came out as scorn, she realised in dismay.

'It can be a very useful asset,' he agreed smoothly.

'It certainly seems to be working wonders for Celeste.' Olivia smiled brightly to prove that she didn't mind the exercising of that charm on another woman or her cousin's totally predictable response.

His eyes narrowed slightly. Was she jealous or just indifferent? The cool, light tone was giving nothing away.

'I've arranged for some other tests,' he told her, quite unnecessarily but wishing to detain her for a few more moments. 'Blood, urine, X-rays . . . all routine investigations, of course. I don't expect to find anything suspicious.'

'We both know that all she really needs is love,' Olivia said lightly.

'She's a very sick girl, whatever the cause,' he returned carefully. He wondered why they were discussing Celeste when he really wanted to suggest that they have lunch and spend the rest of the day together. Usually so confident in his dealings with women, Morgan wasn't at all sure about this one, suddenly so cool and distant and discouraging. It scarcely seemed possible that this was the girl who had gone so eagerly into his arms and shared with him the golden moments of a very memorable lovemaking. 'In the meantime, I don't want her to have any visitors. Even you, Olivia.'

She was dismayed. The 'no visitors' rule was probably very sensible but she was a trained nurse and she wasn't likely to excite her cousin unduly. She looked at him in surprise. 'Does Celeste know?'

Morgan hesitated. Then he decided that it was just as well to be frank. 'Celeste doesn't wish to see you,' he said gently. 'I'm sorry.'

She stared. 'Not wish to see *me*! I don't understand . . .'

'She seems to be feeling rather hostile towards you at present. I don't know why. For no reason at all, probably, except that she's veering between need and rejection of people as a result of her emotional confusion. But if it's going to disturb her to see you, then it's better that you should stay away for the time being.'

Olivia suddenly understood. Somehow, with her unfailing instinct for recognising a rival, Celeste had sensed that she was emotionally involved with Morgan. Naturally jealous and possessive, thoroughly spoiled by the admiration and adulation of too many men, she might not want him for herself but nor did she want him in Olivia's arms.

It wasn't going to happen. But it seemed that Celeste had realised the subtle change in their relationship even if she didn't know exactly what had caused it. She was a very good guesser and Olivia doubted if she had been clever enough to hide her feelings from her too-perceptive cousin.

Celeste knew a sensual man when she met one and she had been suspicious of their possible interest in each other from the start. She was quite devious enough to pretend to believe in the affair with Jean-Paul while knowing perfectly well that it was camouflage.

Now, she possibly felt that by keeping Olivia away from the clinic with a pretence of hostility, she kept her away from Morgan. It was not logical. But Celeste was not in the right frame of mind to think things through just now.

She nodded. 'Very well. She'll have a change of heart tomorrow and demand to know why I haven't been to see her, of course! I shall lay the blame at your door,' she said lightly.

Morgan chuckled. 'My shoulders are broad enough to take it! Why don't you leave those things at the reception desk for your cousin and let me drive you back? I have to make a call in that neighbourhood.'

In truth, it would take him well out of his way but none of his calls were urgent and he welcomed an opportunity to melt her reserve.

Olivia had no good reason to refuse and a very foolish desire to accept. Soon, she was sitting beside him, curls ruffled by the breeze and hands clasped a little tensely in her lap, making rather stilted conversation as the winding ribbon of road disappeared beneath the wheels of his car. He was driving too fast for her liking. In no time at all, they would be at the villa and he would drop her off and drive away—and they wouldn't have exchanged two meaningful words since leaving the clinic!

Travelling along the high coast road that eventually dropped down to the village and beyond, Morgan suddenly slowed the car and then brought it to a standstill before a panoramic view of the sea and the distant headland of Monte Carlo.

'How lovely!' Olivia exclaimed in genuine admiration.

Morgan was admiring her pretty, sun-kissed face and the glints of gold in her soft hair as it reflected sunlight. He had seen the view a thousand times. He was beginning to feel that he could look at her enchanting loveliness for ever and never tire of it. He was beginning to accept that she belonged in his heart and in his life until the end of time.

'Very lovely,' he said softly, meaningfully.

Olivia glanced at him quickly, with the hint of an uncertain smile. Meeting his dark eyes, she sensed the stirring desire, so unwelcome when it was so superficial and so meaningless and such an affront to the way she felt about him. She was immediately on the defensive, ready to ward off even the lightest of lovemaking.

He reached for the ribbon that had slipped from her hair and his long fingers lay briefly against the nape of her neck. A little shudder of tremulous memory rippled down her spine, much to her annoyance. She moved from that too-disturbing touch.

Morgan wound the silk strand of ribbon about his fingers and tucked the neat coil into his breast-pocket. 'A keepsake,' he said, smiling.

'To add to all the other trophies, no doubt,' Olivia returned dryly.

He shook his head. 'I don't collect trophies, as you call them. Most women aren't worth remembering. I happen to think that you are.'

He leaned to kiss her. Olivia drew back hastily. She didn't believe him and she refused to be flattered. He was just an incurable flirt who couldn't resist an opportunity, she thought bitterly. She had been too gullible and too foolish already where he was concerned and she didn't mean to fall into his arms again at the mere lift of a finger!

She laughed. 'With those looks and that glib tongue it isn't surprising that you always get your wicked way with women!' she declared brightly, mocking his charm and her own too-ready response to it. 'No wonder they called you *Beau* at Kit's. According to all I ever heard, you certainly lived up to it!' There was a slight and unmistakable edge to her tone.

'In my medical days, certainly,' Morgan agreed frankly, stifling a protest at her distrust of him and knowing that he must be patient. She was well worth winning and therefore she was well worth waiting for, he reminded himself. 'But you said that you remember me as a registrar. By then, I'd outgrown most of my wildness, you know. I was even planning to get married. Whatever you heard was probably highly exaggerated.'

'But you were sacked!' Olivia exclaimed on a sudden rush of memory. 'You had to leave Kit's in a hurry!' She struggled to remember *why*. Something about a pregnant staff nurse and an abortion and scurrilous speculation on his part in it! Her eyes widened in sudden dismay for she shared every nurse's views on the wanton destruction of new life.

Morgan suddenly tensed and his dark eyes blazed with anger and long-felt bitterness. 'I left at the end of a year's contract as registrar to Professor Lowrie,' he said coldly. 'My departure coincided with certain events. Those events were not responsible for my departure, contrary to rumour. Mud sticks, they say! My God, I didn't expect to be defending myself four years later and on the other side of the Channel!'

He switched on the ignition and started the car, struggling to keep a rein on his temper. He was bitterly disappointed that she was so ready to believe the worst of him like too many of his friends and colleagues during those painful days. He was angry that he had dreamed of persuading her to love him. Love him! He was beginning to doubt that she even liked him—and her obvious recoil proved that she was a million miles away from trusting him!

He took a corner too fast and the lurch of the car threw her against him. She straightened, angry in her turn. 'Are you trying to kill us both?' she demanded. 'Slow down, for heaven's sake!'

'Sorry . . . !' He was curt. He eased his foot a trifle on the accelerator. The car shot down the hill and through the village at considerable speed. It came to a halt outside the Villa Paradis with a squeal of brakes.

Olivia was furious, having been thoroughly scared and thoroughly shocked by his reckless disregard for anything in his path. 'Remind me never to travel in a car with you again!' she flared, struggling with the handle of the door.

'Remind me never to give you the opportunity!' he returned brusquely, leaning to open the door for her.

Olivia scrambled out and turned to the house without another word or a backward glance. The gravel scrunched beneath the wheels of the car—and he was gone.

CHAPTER TEN

OLIVIA was greeted by an excitable Marthe and a flurry of French to which neither her fluency nor her temper were equal at that particular moment. Making neither head nor tail of it, she gave up the attempt to make sense of the tirade.

'*C'est ca! C'est ca!*' she said hastily and brushed past the big woman and into the sitting-room, still shaken and totally unprepared for the man who rose from the sofa where he had been lounging, awaiting her return.

Tall and broad and remarkably handsome, with a distinctive blaze of white against rich auburn hair and vivid blue eyes that were really the first thing that anyone noticed about him, he came towards her with a confident smile of greeting.

Olivia felt as though all the breath had been knocked out of her slight body. Before she could get it back, he had taken her into his arms and kissed her.

'Surprised to see me, aren't you?' he drawled, amused. 'You might look pleased!'

'I'm not!' she said with truth.

He chuckled. 'Darling Olivia, I could always rely on you to speak your mind—and I love you for it!'

She drew away from him and looked at him with a little dislike. 'I wonder if you'll love me quite so much when I've finished speaking my mind! I've an awful lot to say to you and I don't think you're going to like any of it!'

'Darling, you're trembling,' he said gently, obviously

untroubled by look or tone. He took her hands and drew her to sit down with him on the sofa. 'Am I such a shock?'

'Well, of course! I can't think what you're doing here,' she said bluntly. 'When I think of the way you've behaved . . . !'

'Abominably,' he conceded. 'I know.' He carried one of her hands to his lips, a rueful smile in the very blue eyes. 'You could try to forgive me,' he suggested meekly.

Olivia pulled her hand away. 'I can't believe that you care!'

He looked at her steadily. 'Oh, I always valued your good opinion, Olivia. Perhaps more than anyone's.'

'Including your wife,' she said crisply.

Tom nodded. 'Too easily given and never earned. Why should I value it? I had to work for yours, Olivia. I don't think you ever knew how hard I worked for it or what it meant when you eventually relented and decided to like me.'

'It's a pity that you didn't try as hard to be a good husband,' she told him tartly. She had never pulled her punches where he was concerned and she didn't mean to begin now. She was possibly the only person who had never been blinded by his looks and personality and that special gift called charisma which had made him so successful and so popular.

He shrugged. 'Where was the need? I could never do anything wrong in Celeste's eyes. Very flattering. Very boring. Very restricting. I did well to stand it for two years, I think.'

'You should never have married her,' she told him bluntly. 'You knew how she felt about you.'

'I think you know why I married Celeste,' he said after a momentary hesitation. She stiffened at something in his tone. He studied her with an intensity that was slightly disturbing. 'Why didn't you marry your doctor?' he asked abruptly.

Olivia had been dreading the inevitable question. She was terrified of hearing just why he had turned up at the Villa Paradis without warning when she had been so sure that he would not.

'It seems that men are prone to changing their minds,' she said, very carefully, deliberately light.

He frowned. 'The man's a bloody fool! I knew you were wasted on him.' He laid a strong hand on her shoulder. 'Hurt you, did he? I'll punch his nose for him if I ever run into him,' he said with sudden violence.

Olivia knew that he meant it. 'I wish you were as concerned for Celeste's feelings as you are for mine!' she said sharply.

'I don't love Celeste,' he told her, very softly.

Her heart almost stopped at the words. The moment she had been dreading for a very long time seemed to be looming much too near.

Caring for Celeste, concerned for Celeste, she had still been thankful and rather relieved to learn that Tom was sufficiently in love with the pretty Anna Mackintosh to leave his wife for her. The news had lifted a heavy burden from Olivia's mind and heart although it had almost destroyed his wife.

At last, she had found it possible to laugh at the absurd fancy that he was deeply in love with her. So much for feminine intuition, she had derided, delighted. She had even wondered if Celeste was right to believe that eventually she would be the only woman in Tom's life for all the passing fancies.

Now, she was alarmed. She had never wanted Tom to love her. She had never encouraged him by word or glance or deed and perhaps that was one of the reasons why she meant so much to him, she thought shrewdly. A man like Tom would always respond to that kind of challenge.

He had never said that he loved her. much to her heartfelt relief. But a woman knew when a man regarded her with the kind of passionate intensity that someone like Tom would inevitably bring to loving.

If only he could have felt all that passion for the girl he had married, she thought sadly. Poor Celeste! Loving him, living for him, the discovery that Tom only really wanted the cousin that she had turned to for companion and confidante when he went away would probably be the final blow to her emotional and mental stability.

'Don't say it, Tom,' she said quickly, almost desperately, sure that the words were hovering on his lips. 'Please don't say anything!' Once said, they would echo in her mind and heart for ever, a torment to her conscience. For how could she be sure that she had never consciously or unconsciously encouraged him to love her!

He smiled, understanding. He put a hand to her head, cradled it briefly, very tenderly. 'Who needs words?' he agreed. 'Haven't you always known?'

'I don't know anything—and I don't wish to know,' she said, very firm.

His fingers trailed down her cheek in light caress. She understood that he needed to touch her, needed to ease the pressure of his heart with words. Loving Morgan had brought her new and sensitive insight. She felt for Tom. But she was no nearer to caring for him than she had ever been. She liked him. Everyone did. But he was just Tom . . . and for two years he had been her cousin's husband and it had never even occurred to her to want him.

'Still in love with your doctor?' he asked quietly.

It had never been possible for Olivia to lie. She looked at him with candid grey eyes. 'No. I was very fond of him, Tom. But it wasn't love, after all.'

He raised an eyebrow. 'You've discovered the difference?'

She was quick to disillusion him, hearing the slight quickening of hope in his voice. 'Yes, I have. That doesn't mean that I'm in love with you,' she said deliberately.

'Or ever will be,' he said, accepting.

'Or ever will be,' she underlined.

'Stubborn and loyal to the end, aren't you? Maybe if I hadn't married Celeste . . .' He broke off, mouth tightening. 'You have so much integrity, darling,' he went on lightly.

'If only I could say the same for you,' she returned with a slight smile.

'It's very strange that the only woman who has ever really loved me is as blind as a bat to all my faults,' he said dryly.

Olivia laughed. 'Perhaps that's why she loves you!'

'Maybe,' he agreed, rueful.

She was suddenly serious. 'But it isn't true, Tom. She does see your faults. Some of them make her very unhappy. But she loves you, anyway. Stubborn loyalty runs in the family, you see.'

'Where is she?' he asked with belated interest. 'My

French isn't terribly good but I think the maid said something about a sanatorium. Is Celeste still ill?'

'She has been very ill. She's much better but she's gone into a local clinic for tests.' Olivia hesitated. 'Do you know, she was so sure that you would come. I just didn't believe it. That's why you were such a shock.'

'I heard that you were with Celeste,' he said bluntly. 'Then I made some enquiries and learned that you'd left St Christopher's—and why! I came to see you, Olivia.'

'No!' she retorted, very sharply. 'You came to see Celeste! You came because you couldn't stay away any longer!'

'That's true, certainly,' he murmured, wry.

She turned her head to look at him. 'She needs you so much, Tom,' she said gently. 'Perhaps you need each other.' Two unhappy people, both wanting something they might never have, could possibly comfort each other, she felt. At the very back of her mind lay the unadmitted knowledge that he had married Celeste as a substitute for her. In some ways they were alike, although she was a very pale copy of Celeste's glowing beauty and exciting personality. He might have chafed at the bonds of Celeste's love, but no doubt he needed it more than he knew. In time, he might value it much more than the elusive love that Olivia would never feel for him.

Tom leaned forward, hands locked between his knees. He was silent, very tense. Olivia saw the nerve jumping in his jaw and the whiteness of the strong knuckles as his hands clenched.

She saw how he battled with the force of his emotions in those few moments and it frightened her that any man should feel so strongly about her. At the same time, she wished with all her heart that Morgan loved her with so much passion, so much intensity of longing and need. With a little ache at her heart, she thought she understood why Tom had turned to Celeste who loved him, why he had married her . . . and even why he had hurt her again and again during the two years that they had been together. He had settled for second best and despised himself for it. His wife's continued love despite everything shamed him and so he had done all he could to lose it.

For several moments, the atmosphere in the room was electric. Olivia didn't dare to speak or move although her compassionate heart longed to reach out and comfort him.

Then he relaxed. Raising his head, he smiled at her—and Olivia relaxed. He had obviously reached a decision. 'Back to square one,' he said with a shrug that accepted the inevitable.

Olivia nodded, understanding.

They went out to his car to bring in his luggage now that it was tacitly understood that he would be staying. Olivia wondered that she hadn't noticed the distinctive yellow car with its personalised number plate, TK 1, and then recalled that she hadn't been in the mood to notice anything when she rushed into the house.

Hastily thrusting Morgan from her thoughts, she invited Tom to admire the Villa Paradis in its very attractive surroundings. It was another perfect day of blue skies and bright sunshine and soon it would be so hot that they would be glad of the shade from the tall palm trees.

Olivia pointed out various features and Tom looked and pretended to listen and smiled at her with a very tender light in his blue eyes. He put an arm about her shoulders and dropped a kiss on her hair and she smiled, sensing that there was only affection in his embrace. Nothing had been said or done that either of them could regret. Celeste need never know that it was not loving concern for her that brought him back, Olivia thought thankfully.

'An angel in Paradise,' Tom said, amused, thinking it a very apt description. For nurses were often described as angels and this lovely place lived up to its name.

Olivia laughed up at him, delighted, quick to grasp the connotation. 'Not a very good angel,' she said deprecatingly.

'Too good for my liking,' he said wryly—and kissed her.

It was the briefest and most gentle of kisses, hinting at loving and need and acceptance of the situation. Olivia was startled but she could not really object when there was not even the hint of an unwelcome passion in the touch of his lips. She put her hand to his head, very fleetingly, in a caress born of caring and compassion rather than the slightest stirring of love.

She drew away from him and turned with that sudden, inexplicable sensation at the back of her neck that told her of Morgan's presence. He stood by the house, some slight distance away, studying them with a little blaze of anger in his dark eyes.

Her heart faltered. She knew he had seen that kiss and placed quite the wrong interpretation on it. She started towards him, abruptly abandoning Tom. Morgan turned on his heel and began to walk towards his car which had glided so silently into the drive that neither she nor Tom had heard its approach.

Olivia ran, caught at his arm. 'Don't go, Morgan. It's

Tom . . . Celeste's husband!' she said in eager explanation.

He paused, looked at her with a smouldering contempt. 'Yes,' he said coldly. 'Marthe told me he was here.'

Having had time to calm down, he had driven back to the villa to see Olivia, to apologise, to make amends. He had been greeted by a voluble Marthe and he had been delighted with the news that Tom Knight had arrived that morning to see his wife. It was just the medicine that Celeste needed, he felt.

Marthe had pointed out the couple in the grounds and he had begun to walk towards them, anxious to meet Knight and to find out for himself what manner of man he really was, ready to relax his embargo on visitors in his case. Then he had seen the man slip an arm about Olivia and draw her towards him. He had seen the exchange of warm glances and warm words with all their obvious meaning. He had seen that kiss with its unmistakable implication. He had felt all the force of a fury such as he had never known before and suddenly understood how murders could be committed in the name of love.

Now, he looked at Olivia and marvelled at her convincing pretence of genuine affection and concern for Celeste when she was so obviously one of the causes of her unhappiness. She was in love with her cousin's husband and contriving to win him for herself. She was a wanton lie from beginning to end, he thought bitterly.

'Come and meet Tom,' Olivia said, her hand falling from his arm as she flinched from the anger in his eyes. She knew she must pretend to be unaware of his fury and his contempt. This was not the moment for explanations. He was in no mood to listen.

'If you're sure it's a convenient moment,' he said, rather grimly.

Olivia smiled. 'Yes, of course. I was only showing him round the garden. I'm so glad you came back, Morgan. I meant to telephone to tell you about Tom. Isn't it marvellous that he's here?'

For Celeste—or for herself, he wondered, observing the eager excitement, the shining eyes, the quick rise and fall of the lovely breasts.

'Time will tell,' he said, cryptically.

Olivia looked at him quickly—and wondered how she could be so stupid! Of course he wasn't at all pleased! He wasn't angry because Tom had kissed her, as she had so foolishly supposed, heart leaping at the hope of jealousy on his part. He was furious because Tom had come to claim the wife who still loved him despite everything!

The two men shook hands, assessing each other. Tom sensed hostility beneath the cool courtesy and professional manner of the doctor. Morgan sensed the man's indifference to his wife's condition and was all the more convinced that Knight had come to the South of France in search of Olivia who had welcomed him with open arms.

Tempted to take the man apart with his bare hands, Morgan was forced to behave like a civilised doctor instead of a jealous savage. He reminded himself that loving Olivia didn't give him any right to resent her obvious preference for Knight, so marked in the way she had reacted to his arrival at the villa.

Bitterly disappointed in her, he knew that he still loved her. She might not be the woman he had so trustingly believed her to be but she was still the only woman he wanted.

He stayed only just long enough to give a brief resumé of Celeste's state of mind and health and to agree that her husband might visit her that afternoon. Then he left.

Olivia accompanied him to his car, sensing his impatience to be gone but feeling that she must try to bridge the widening gulf between them. That night in his arms was rapidly retreating into the dim world of the might-never-have-been, she thought unhappily.

'Do you mean to tell Celeste?' she asked curiously. 'Or just let Tom surprise her?'

'I'm not sure. Why does he wish to see her? He isn't very convincing in the rôle of repentant husband,' he said. 'I doubt if it will do her the slightest good to see him.'

He was too perceptive, Olivia thought. A man in love could sense a rival—and he obviously knew that Tom wasn't at all in love with his wife. So he didn't regard him as a threat on that score. But Celeste loved Tom and she would forgive him anything and take him back instantly, shattering all Morgan's hopes for his happiness.

'Only Tom knows his reasons for returning to Celeste,' she said quietly. 'I think he needs her. She certainly needs him. They are still husband and wife, Morgan. It's just unfortunate that other people have to get hurt in these situations . . .' Not daring to say more, protecting his pride and her own, she smiled at him warmly with a hint of sympathy in her grey eyes.

Morgan didn't recognise it as compassion. He thought it was courage. He thought she was bravely facing up to the hurt of Knight's decision to return to his wife. He wondered if that kiss had been a farewell to all her hopes and dreams of happiness with a man she loved.

He didn't think that Knight cared for Olivia. He wasn't the type to care for anyone other than himself. Recalling the way that she had looked and smiled and raised her hand so lovingly to the man's head when she kissed him, Morgan didn't doubt that Olivia cared for Tom Knight.

He longed to put his arms about her and tell her that he loved her, that he would always be there if she needed him, that he was prepared to wait until the end of time for her to love him. Looking into the wide grey eyes, so deceptively candid that all the anger and bitterness rose in him again, he stifled the impulse and the words.

Olivia was an enigma. He would never know why she had been so ardently responsive in his arms when she obviously cared nothing for him. He had believed that she was grieving for the loss of the man she had loved. Now he doubted that she had ever loved the fiancé who had apparently changed his mind about marrying her at almost the last moment. He had thought that she might be falling in love with Jean-Paul. Now he wondered if she had only been using her friendship with the composer to hurt him for reasons of her own. He had admired her devotion to Celeste and the seemingly genuine concern and compassion. Now he wondered what part she had really played in the near-collapse of her cousin's marriage.

He swung himself into the driving seat and said brusquely: 'If people are foolish enough to get involved in such situations, then perhaps they deserve to be hurt.'

He didn't want her sympathy, Olivia realised with swift understanding that discounted the curtness of his tone and manner. He would rather she didn't know how he felt about Celeste. Well, that was very natural. She didn't want him to know that she loved him and longed for him, after all. Everyone had to hide behind their pride on occasions.

She put a tentative hand on his arm. 'Even fools need friends, Morgan,' she said quietly. It was as near as she dared to telling him that she was there if he wanted her, now or at any time in the future.

Morgan stiffened. It was an obvious plea, but he couldn't feel that this was the right moment for her to make it or him to respond to it. Later, he might be able to give her the comfort and consolation she needed. Just now, he didn't find it easy to swallow his pride and play the part of substitute lover.

He couldn't let her down, of course. He loved her and there was a great deal of genuine need in her voice and eyes and the touch of her hand. But he needed a little time to come to terms with this new Olivia who bore only slight resemblance to the girl who had captured his heart so swiftly.

'I'll remember,' he said carefully. 'I'll be in touch . . .'

The car moved away on the words.

Olivia turned into the house, wondering if he would ever take her up on that heartfelt offer. He had known Celeste such a very short time. Surely he couldn't be so irrevocably in love with her cousin that he couldn't care for someone else one day . . . her, perhaps? If she was very loving, very patient—and if she made a point of being around in his life for some time to come?

He had suggested that she should work at the clinic when Celeste no longer needed her, she reminded herself with fast-beating heart. Surely Celeste wasn't going to need her much longer now that Tom was back to restore her health and spirits to their former high level?

She had nothing to take her back to England. Why shouldn't she apply for a job as a nurse at the Beauclerc Clinic? As a Kit's nurse, she had all the right qualifications . . .

CHAPTER ELEVEN

Tom brought his wife back to the Villa Paradis two days later. Celeste had wanted to leave the clinic immediately to be with him at the villa, declaring that she felt perfectly well. He had insisted that she should stay for the arranged tests and the results. Revelling in his sudden and so unexpected concern for her, she had meekly agreed and all the tests had proved to be negative or wholly reassuring.

Entering the house on Tom's arm, she was as lovely and as radiant as a new bride. Whatever he had said to her since his arrival, however he had convinced her that he was back to stay, it had obviously given her new confidence for the future. She was so quietly happy that it would be a very hard heart that couldn't rejoice for her, Olivia felt.

She kissed her cousin in warm welcome. 'You look marvellous!' she declared. 'I could use a few days at that clinic if it sends every patient home looking as you do!'

'I had a very good doctor,' Celeste said lightly with a loving glance for Tom. 'And the best medicine in the world.'

No one could have been more devoted or more attentive during the last two days. Tom had spent most of every day with his wife, either in her very comfortable room or in the grounds of the clinic.

Olivia had stayed away, knowing that Celeste didn't need anyone but Tom, and afraid that Morgan might feel that she was pursuing him if she continued to haunt the place unnecessarily. He hadn't telephoned her. He hadn't called at the villa to see her. She just didn't seem to exist any more for him. It hurt, dreadfully.

She might have packed her things and gone back to England, in different circumstances. But she couldn't leave when she loved Morgan so much and might yet play some small part in his life. She meant to make formal application through the usual channels for a job at the clinic and she had already made some enquiries. Celeste would be returning to England with Tom in the very near future, apparently. He was due to begin shooting on a new film in which he was to play one of the leading rôles. Olivia hoped to stay on at the villa, improving her French, until she moved into staff quarters at the clinic.

Celeste went out to the terrace to look at the sea. Olivia smiled at Tom, very warm, very approving and took the opportunity to murmur: 'She's so happy, Tom. All she ever needed was loving.'

He smiled wryly. 'It isn't easy.'

'Don't you think she knows that?' Olivia said promptly. 'She values it all the more! Any woman would!'

'She hasn't reproached me,' he told her, a little dryly. 'She's been very generous about Anna. She oozes with forgiveness.'

'She *has* forgiven you, I expect. That's loving.'

'She could have let me go. That's loving, too!'

'She was letting you go,' Olivia reminded him swiftly. 'She was giving you the divorce you wanted although it was destroying her! She wanted you desperately but she didn't ask you to come back—not once! That wasn't pride. That was not standing in the way of the happiness that you thought you could find with someone else!'

'I *could* have found it with someone else,' Tom said softly, meaningfully. He took a step towards her, held out his hand on a sudden impulse of love and longing. 'It isn't too late . . .'

She shook her head at him in swift warning. His hand dropped to his side as Celeste appeared in the open frame of the long window. She looked from her husband to her cousin, smiling.

'Are we having tea on the terrace? It's a lovely afternoon,' she said, eyes and voice so serene that neither suspected that she had witnessed that small tableau and heard his heartcry. 'You didn't tell me that Jean-Paul was back, Olivia.'

'I didn't know.' She felt a flicker of surprise that he had arrived without telling her and then reminded herself that she really had no claim on him. She went towards the window. 'Is he on the beach?' If she had been more alert, she might have sensed the way in which Celeste seemed to shrink back from her as she went out to the terrace and certainly she ought to have remembered that Celeste always shortened her name to *Livvy*. Her full name on her cousin's lips should have struck a warning note.

She saw Jean-Paul in the familiar, brightly coloured shorts, his blond curls gleaming in the sun, and waved to him as he chanced to glance in her direction. She was glad that he was back at last. It was only a few days since she had seen him, of course. It seemed very much longer.

He waved in reply but didn't immediately cross the beach towards her as she had expected. She glanced over her shoulder. Celeste had gone into the house. Olivia opened the little gate in the wall and stepped down to the beach and began to walk across the golden sand.

She was feeling distinctly *de trop* at the moment. Tom and Celeste had a great deal of catching-up to do and they certainly didn't need to have her around to play gooseberry. Besides, Tom had not yet settled down completely to the thought of staying with Celeste and it seemed to unsettle him more because she was about.

He had behaved well since his arrival, very circumspect, very controlled, and Olivia hadn't had to keep him at arms' length as she had feared. She had been thankful. It wasn't comfortable to be under the same roof with a man who felt so strongly about her and made it clear without words. She couldn't help a little anxiety that passion might suddenly break the bonds of restraint. Now that she knew how powerful a force it could be, she realised the danger of even the smallest encouragement of his feelings and she had been constantly on edge whenever he was in the house.

Fortunately, he had spent most of his time at the clinic with Celeste. Now, she didn't understand why he had suddenly moved towards her with that particular look in his very blue eyes and that unmistakable hunger in his deep voice just when Celeste was hovering on the terrace and all the good of the last few days might be undone. She supposed it must be a strain for him to play the rôle of devoted husband to one woman when he longed constantly for another. She sympathised—and knew that she would find it a great relief when he and Celeste left the villa.

Jean-Paul moved to meet her, smiling.

She hugged him, impulsively. 'I'm so glad to see you, Jean-Paul!' she said warmly.

He kissed her cheek, light and friendly. 'How are

you . . . and Madame?'

She thought he was slightly guarded in his manner. Perhaps he had come too near to caring for her and didn't mean it to happen again. He was just the same—but different. She felt a rush of warm affection for him and it showed in her eyes and voice as she declared: 'She's well—and happy! She was right, after all, Jean-Paul! Her husband came to see her and they're together again. Isn't it marvellous?'

'*Incroyable!* I am happy for them!' he said with genuine delight. He looked at her pretty face and sparkling eyes and added: 'And you, Olivia. You are—happy?'

Olivia knew that he referred obliquely to her feeling for Morgan. He knew the extent of her involvement with the doctor, none better! He had gone away rather than watch its progress, she believed. It was humiliating to have none to report . . . and hurtful, she thought wryly.

'For Celeste? Oh, of course!' she exclaimed, deliberately misunderstanding. 'I never thought it could happen.' She slipped her hand into his arm. 'Are you busy? Come and say hallo to Celeste—and meet Tom!'

He hesitated.

A girl came to the door of his villa, very young and very pretty, long black hair cascading to her waist in tousled waves and curls. A bright towel had been hastily and skimpily wrapped about a nude and nubile body and she had obviously just got out of bed. She was flushed and yawning with a delicious languour that told its own story. She looked down at them from the top of the steps and spoke to Jean-Paul in very rapid French.

Slightly embarrassed and ridiculously dismayed, Olivia drew her hand slowly from his arm, suddenly realising the possessiveness in the link and how easily it could be misconstrued by the girl.

'Come later . . .' she said awkwardly. 'Come for drinks—and bring your friend.' She smiled at the girl in friendly fashion, annoyed with herself for even that small flicker of quite unnecessary jealousy.

'Come down and be introduced, Madeleine,' Jean-Paul ordered in his own language. 'This is the English nurse that I told you about.' He turned back to Olivia. 'Madeleine is a dancer, but she has a passion for nursing. She wants to go to England to train but she says that she has never heard of Kit's. That is the name of your hospital, isn't it?'

'St Christopher's!' She laughed. 'Oh, I'm sorry, Jean-Paul. Kit's is just an affectionate name for it used by the staff. I'll be pleased to tell her anything that she wants to know, of course.' Her eyes were suddenly alive with merriment. 'I've always longed to be a dancer. Absurd, isn't it?' she exclaimed lightly.

Madeleine descended the steps in mingled shyness and suspicion. But within a very few minutes, she was plying Olivia with eager questions in fluent English and she was promising to do what she could to help her to achieve her ambition. She knew that girls arrived from all over the world to train at St Christopher's, one of the best and most respected of the famous London teaching hospitals that still maintained the old traditions and disciplines despite the grumbles of the progressives.

Jean-Paul sat on the steps and listened. Olivia felt the warmth of his gaze on her face and, glancing at him, found a lingering of the affection and admiration that might have become loving if the chemistry had been right between them. She felt a familiar tug of regret that it couldn't have been Jean-Paul who had swept her into loving. Loving Morgan didn't seem to hold any promise of happiness, after all. He was a stranger. Come what may, Jean-Paul would remain a very dear friend, she felt.

Repeating the invitation to drinks for that evening, she left them and made her way to rejoin Tom and Celeste.

Tea had already been brought out to the terrace. Tom lay at full length on a lounger, a drink in his hand. 'Where's Celeste?' Olivia asked quickly.

'In her room.'

'Is she all right?'

He shrugged. 'Tired, she says.'

'Tired!' Olivia couldn't believe it. Her cousin had been quiet but obviously in perfect health, blooming with radiance and glowing with happiness. She looked at Tom doubtfully. 'You haven't quarrelled?' she asked anxiously.

He looked at her steadily. 'Darling, I'm a reformed character. Would I quarrel with my lovely wife?'

'Please be serious!'

He raised an eyebrow. 'Innocent, me lud!'

She turned away from him, impatiently. If only he really cared! She was suddenly despondent, doubting if all his efforts could save their marriage when there was so little heart behind them and wondering why he bothered at all! It couldn't be to please her!

She knocked lightly on Celeste's bedroom door and entered. Her cousin was sitting in a chair by the window. She didn't turn or speak or smile and Olivia felt an odd disquiet. She had the strange feeling that she was looking at the shell of someone who had gone away. Celeste was so still, so remote, no flicker of animation in the lovely face and a disturbing blankness in the beautiful violet eyes.

She touched the slender shoulder. Celeste didn't seem to notice. 'Didn't you want any tea?' she asked gently.

'No.'

The flat, too-quiet monosyllable seemed to speak volumes to Olivia, so sensitive to her cousin's moods. She bent down and put an arm about her, concerned, comforting. 'What is it, darling?'

Celeste didn't yield or stiffen. She merely sat like a crumpled doll, drained of all vitality. 'I'm tired. I want to rest. Go and talk to Tom.'

'Shall I help you to undress? Lie down for an hour and I'm sure you'll be fine. Jean-Paul is coming for cocktails and you'll want to see him, won't you?'

'I don't need you. Go and talk to Tom.'

Olivia straightened, reluctant to leave her, anxious not to play the nurse if it was no longer necessary. It had become a habit to worry about her cousin, she knew. She mustn't allow her imagination to run away with her just because Celeste wished to sit quietly in her room for a while. Perhaps she was tired, in fact, not from exertion but from the stress of recent events. Perhaps she needed a brief breathing-space to adjust to her newfound happiness. Perhaps it was all just a little too much to take when she had been living with despair for weeks. Perhaps it was just reaction.

'All right,' she agreed, moving towards the door. 'We can talk later. I don't have to tell you how happy I am for you, do I? I'm so glad things have worked out right, after all.'

Celeste didn't answer. Glancing at her, Olivia thought

she saw the lovely mouth quiver in a faint smile. Reassured, she went from the room.

As she passed through the hall, the telephone rang. She reached out a hand to lift the receiver, gave the number.

'Morgan Beauclerc,' he announced without preliminary. 'How is Mrs Knight?'

Olivia controlled her leaping heart with an effort, found her voice. 'Hallo, Morgan. It's Olivia,' she said brightly. 'Celeste is rather tired but seems to be fine.' There was nothing in his manner to confirm the absurd hope that he had telephoned to talk to her rather than to enquire after his patient, she thought bleakly.

'Don't let her overdo things,' he warned. 'She's been through a lot of emotional strain and I'm not satisfied that she's really ready to cope with any more.'

Olivia felt a pang at the continued concern that was so much more than professional interest. 'I'll keep a careful eye on her,' she promised. She hesitated. 'I hoped to see you,' she added carefully, anxious not to seem eager but so desperately missing him that she could swallow some of her pride.

'Your cousin is still my patient. I shall be calling to see her during the next day or so,' he returned smoothly.

'I meant . . . not professionally.' Olivia forced the words past reluctant lips in the face of his coolly impersonal tone.

It seemed an eternity of silence before he spoke and then she almost didn't hear the quiet words for the drumming of her anxious heart. 'You could have dinner with me tonight . . . *not professionally*,' he said lightly.

Her face burned at the hint of gentle mockery behind the words. Had she been so obvious? Was she throwing herself at him all over again and just as blatantly as before?

'I'd like that,' she agreed, equally light. Then, afraid that she had leaped too readily at the invitation she had prompted out of him, she added brightly: 'Anything to escape for a few hours! You can imagine what it's like. Morgan!'

'Anything to oblige,' he drawled dryly. 'I'll call for you at eight . . .'

He rang off before Olivia could protest that she had changed her mind. He couldn't really want to see her! She had forced herself on him! It was days since he had seen or spoken to her and it must be obvious to the most insensitive person that he was completely indifferent. What on earth had possessed her to embarrass him and humiliate herself in such fashion, she wondered despairingly.

Tom regarded her from the doorway of the sitting-room. He had been listening quite blatantly to her side of the conversation, she realised. There was a hint of challenge in the way she looked at him, the way her chin tilted before the slight smile in his very blue eyes.

'Another doctor,' he commented, mocking. 'You seem to be turned on by white coats, darling. What's wrong with actors, I wonder?'

'Nothing at all—when they aren't playing a part off the stage as well as on,' she returned, rather tart because she was slightly on the defensive.

His eyes narrowed. 'I thought you meant me to play a part, Olivia. God knows I'm loathing every minute of it! Shall I be myself and tell the world what I really think and feel about this bloody charade for your sake?'

She stepped back before the blaze of anger in his

brilliant eyes and the passion of his angry words. 'I'm not running your life, Tom,' she said quietly. 'You must do what you really want to do. I just wanted Celeste to be happy.'

'At my expense!'

'Oh, hush!' she said anxiously, glancing along the hall to the closed door of Celeste's bedroom. 'Do you want her to hear? Do you want her to know how little you care? Why didn't you just go away again and let the divorce go through and give her the chance to make a new life with someone else? It would have happened in time!' She brushed past him, rather angry. 'You're the most selfish man I've ever known. You want the best of both worlds!'

He caught her wrist and pulled her towards him, jerking her off balance so that she almost fell against him. He promptly put his arms about her, ignoring her murmur of protest. Olivia stood rigid, hands hard against his chest, defiance in her grey eyes and protest in every line of her slender body. She looked up at him steadily, daring him to make love to her by word or deed at the risk of alienating her for ever. She saw the inclination in his eyes and sensed the tension in his tall body and resisted him with all her will.

He released her abruptly. He was breathing hard, fighting for control. 'I want you,' he said unsteadily. 'I'm a selfish brute and I need you, Olivia. Come away with me. I can't go on without you. She'll get over it, find someone else, just as you said. I can't and won't lose you!'

She saw and heard his anguish. He trembled with the force of his emotions. It was impossible to doubt that he meant every word. She looked at him sadly.

'I'm sorry, Tom. I never wanted this to happen,' she said gently. 'I don't want it now. You ask the impossible.' She had to be honest. There was no other way for someone like Olivia. 'One of us has to go,' she added wryly, quite determined. 'Celeste needs you. So it will have to be me. You've made it too difficult for us both to be beneath the same roof, I'm afraid.'

'That's ridiculous . . . !' he began impatiently.

She cut him short. 'That's common-sense! I'm not going to risk what will happen to Celeste if she finds out how you feel!'

'What do you suppose she'll think if you go away, for heaven's sake!' he demanded.

'She won't think that you've had any part in it, I promise you,' Olivia returned, rather dryly.

She left him and hurried to her room before he could demand to know what she was planning to do . . .

She might have gone to Jean-Paul, confident that he would understand and be willing to help her. But it would be asking too much of him just now in view of his relationship with Madeleine. She had no right to spoil things for him in that direction. So there was only Morgan.

Later, failing to find Celeste in her room, she went in search of her and found her with Tom in the sitting-room.

She was seated at the piano, singing softly to herself while lightly picking out the notes of a favourite love song. She had dressed for dinner and looked particularly lovely in rose-coloured velvet, her pale hair framing her beautiful face. She looked very serene. She looked as if she was in an enchanted world of her own, Olivia thought, slightly envious but glad that Tom could be so convincing despite his true feelings. He was an actor, of course. Olivia forgot that Celeste was an actress, too.

Tom was sprawled in a chair with a glass in his hand and a half-empty bottle of whisky on the low table by his side. Olivia felt a slight qualm. But his blue eyes were sober enough as he regarded her, unsmiling and rather bleak. She looked away, all the more convinced that she was doing the right thing in removing herself from his orbit.

She had never known him to be drunk, she reassured herself. Perhaps he needed a certain amount of whisky to dull the pain of loving the wrong woman, she thought wryly, thankful that Celeste didn't know the truth. She hoped devoutly that she would never know.

It seemed unlikely that Tom could be any more content with his wife than he had been for the past two years. But acceptance of the futility of loving Olivia might persuade him to stay married to someone who loved him and asked little of him, she thought hopefully.

'You haven't changed,' Celeste said slowly, painstakingly uttering the words and looking at Olivia as if she had only just become aware of her presence in the room.

At any other time, Olivia would have noticed the strangeness of her manner, the slight slurring of the words and the flatness of the usually lilting voice and suspected that Celeste had also been drinking. But her mind was rather full of other things just then and she had already ceased to think of her cousin as a patient who needed her concern and attention.

'Not yet,' she returned lightly. 'I'm going out. I thought that it would be nice for you and Tom to have the evening on your own and my love life has been sadly neglected just lately.' She smiled at Celeste, ignoring

Tom's slight scowl at the bright words.

Celeste nodded, fingers already straying over the keys in search of another song. Olivia doubted if she had even heard. It didn't matter. Celeste was on cloud number seven just now—and that was how it should be, she thought thankfully, relieved by her cousin's obvious contentment and newfound peace of mind.

Later, with Tom's arms about her, she wouldn't know or care that Olivia hadn't returned from her dinner date . . .

CHAPTER TWELVE

Olivia packed quickly and methodically, not really sorry to be leaving the Villa Paradis for all its luxury and lovely surroundings.

She dressed carefully for her evening with Morgan, choosing to wear a long black skirt with appliqued velvet roses and a filmy black blouse with deeply-scooped neckline and long, flowing sleeves. It was an elegant and flattering outfit, complementing her creamy complexion and the gold-flecked chestnut hair.

She piled her curls into a knot high on her head and bound them with a black velvet band. She made up eyes and mouth with special care and felt that she was looking her best when she finally sat back to study her reflection in the dressing-table mirror.

Eyes were slightly too bright and mouth slightly too tremulous, perhaps. But that was due to mingled excitement and apprehension. For she was about to throw herself on the mercy of Morgan's good nature and she didn't know how he would react.

She was waiting for the first glimpse of the car some time before it turned through the white gates and approached the house.

With her heart hammering in her throat, she went towards him, carrying case and bag and topcoat, and saw the flicker of surprise in his eyes. She was suddenly alarmed by the enormity of what she proposed to do. He was a stranger, after all—and she didn't even know what he felt about her!

But it was too late to turn back.

'I'm not coming back!' she said quickly, breathlessly. 'I can't! May I stay with you for a day or two? I haven't anyone else to ask!'

Morgan took the heavy case from her hand and put a reassuring arm about her slender shoulders, smiling into the slightly anxious eyes. 'Of course,' he said simply. He thought he understood her need to escape. Her cousin's obvious happiness probably emphasised her own disappointment. He was glad that Olivia had turned to him for some degree of consolation and comfort. It might so easily have been Jean-Paul.

Olivia's heart steadied. She had known that he wouldn't let her down, she thought thankfully—and that was odd when she recalled how mistrustful of him she had felt when they first met. Now, she might not know very much more about him, but she did trust him and she knew that she loved him and always would. That was all that really mattered, she felt.

'I'm very grateful,' she said warmly.

He stored her case in the boot of his car. 'It's the least I can do for a Kit's nurse,' he said lightly.

Olivia looked up at him doubtfully. 'I didn't think you felt very kindly towards Kit's.'

'I don't . . . with very good reason. But that doesn't mean that I can't do a good turn for one of its prettiest nurses,' he told her, smiling.

She was silenced, blushing. It would be nice to believe that she really was so pretty in his eyes, she thought wistfully.

Morgan settled her comfortably in the car beside him.

As they drove away from the Villa Paradis, he observed that she didn't glance back. He admired her ability to put the past behind her. It gave him some slight hope for the future.

'What are your plans?' he asked gently. 'I understand that the Knights are going back to England next week. Do you go with them?' He tried to keep a very natural anxiety from his tone.

'I don't think so.' She smiled at him. 'I like this part of the world . . . and the people! You may remember that you suggested I should work at the clinic when Celeste was well—and that's what I'm hoping to do, in fact. But perhaps you weren't serious?'

'Of course I was serious! I'm very pleased,' he said swiftly. 'We need you at the clinic. My theatre nurse hasn't been really well for some time and I've just learned that she has been advised to have a hysterectomy. So you'd be a marvellous replacement at just the right time, Olivia!'

'It's something I'd like to do,' she admitted, remembering how well they had worked together in the theatre, blessed with a very necessary rapport. 'But I don't know if my French is good enough . . .'

'It will improve,' he said firmly. He reached for one of her hands, lying in her lap, pressed it warmly. 'I'll teach you myself—and I know you to be a very quick learner,' he added with a little imp of mischief in his dark eyes.

Olivia laughed, very relaxed. Suddenly she knew that the evening was going to be a success. He did like her still, she thought with a little lift of her heart. Something still sparked between them despite the shadow of Celeste. Perhaps one day it would ignite a more lasting flame than a fleeting and unreliable desire.

'Where are we going?' she asked curiously as he took the winding coast road instead of the way through the village towards the clinic.

'I thought I'd introduce you to some friends who run a rather nice restaurant. It isn't far and I can guarantee the food. I think you'll like the scenery, too . . .'

Olivia was glad that she had dressed with special care for the evening when they arrived at the small but very exclusive restaurant that nestled on the side of the hill overlooking the sea. The place was filled with beautiful and elegant women with their attentive and well-dressed escorts and heads turned as she entered on Morgan's arm. She was glad that she was looking reasonably chic and even felt that she might be looking pretty. Morgan had a gift for making a woman feel that she was attractive and desirable, she had discovered.

He was not only distinctive and attractive but also very well known in the district. Several people nodded or smiled or spoke a friendly greeting. Twin brothers, Jules and Dominic St Pier, ran the restaurant very successfully. Only Jules was present that night and he insisted that they should have a drink with him at the bar before they were ushered to one of the best tables with its superb view of the sea and the coastline.

Olivia was very impressed and said so in impulsive and genuine appreciation. Morgan smiled at her across the candlelit table. 'I'm glad you like it. This is my usual table, but we were very lucky to get it at such short notice. The advantage of having friends in high places, you see!'

She laughed at the drollery. But she wondered if he had brought many women to this enchanting place with its soft lighting and background music and the intimate atmosphere that was so conducive to a romantic evening.

There must have been so many women in his life—and she couldn't be the only one to have fallen in love with him. She didn't resent the unknown women in his past, but she couldn't help a pang at the thought that she might not play a very important part in his future.

Very handsome, very impressive, disturbingly attractive in dark-blue dinner jacket and powder-blue dress shirt, dark hair gleaming in the candlelight and a ready smile in the depths of his dark eyes, he was the kind of man that women inevitably noticed and desired. It was not just his good looks or his charm or his physical magnetism. There was a warmth and a strength and a depth to him that stirred liking and admiration and respect as much as physical attraction.

Olivia didn't understand how he could have left Kit's under any kind of a cloud. He admitted that he had been a rake and a devil-may-care who had enjoyed scandalising the authorities to some extent. But there was no way that he could have been involved in something as despicable as the illegal abortion of an unwanted pregnancy, she felt. He had too much integrity and too much respect for the Hippocratic Oath. He had denied all responsibility and Olivia knew that she believed him. She could understand the fierce pride that had forbidden him to put up any kind of defence in the face of false accusation from those he had believed to be his friends. She could understand his hurt and his bitterness. She could understand and sympathise with the still-simmering anger. No wonder he was not too inclined to give too much of himself to a Kit's nurse, she thought ruefully. She stirred too many painful memories.

Olivia enjoyed that evening. The food and the wine were really excellent. She was relaxed, happy to be with Morgan and able to forget everything else. The touch of his hand was magic. Dancing with him was sheer delight, another memory to treasure. They moved slowly and sensuously to the music, his cheek pressed to her soft hair, just a hint of tension in the way that he held her, not too close but with tenderness. Olivia's heart swelled as she danced in those strong and seemingly secure arms. She knew that she would love him for the rest of her life and wished that she had the courage to say so.

Instead, she talked of a hundred other things that evening . . . talked rather too much, perhaps, she thought wryly, wondering if he suspected why she skated over everything but the superficial. She thought she must betray her feeling for him with every glance, every smile, every light touch of her hand. She knew she touched him too often, laying her hand on his arm, allowing their fingers to brush, putting a hand to his lean cheek in impulsive caress whenever he made her laugh or murmured something complimentary. But she desperately needed the physical contact—and she needed the reassurance in the lack of rebuff.

She knew that the evening was steadily building towards its inevitable ending—and she was glad. She could make him want her despite all the Celestes in the world, she thought with a flicker of triumph as she caught just a glimpse of a familiar and welcome glow in his eyes.

He had taken her out to the verandah to point out the myriad lights of Monte Carlo on the far distant horizon. They leaned against the wooden rail, side by side, not quite touching.

The moon was riding high that night, full and luminous and breathtakingly beautiful as it emerged from a dark velvet bank of clouds. A lovers moon, Olivia thought wistfully, watching it sail across the night sky and wishing it could stir Morgan's emotions as much as her own.

Ignoring the glory of the moon, Morgan's gaze rested on the woman by his side with very warm and admiring appreciation of a more important loveliness to him.

Soon, he must take her back to his flat . . . and that was going to be a very great strain on his control, he knew. She was too much temptation for any man, so lovely, so feminine, stirring him to fierce and hungry wanting. He didn't even dare to hope that she might want to lie in his arms and give herself to him once more with that glad and endearing delight.

Olivia turned her head, smiled. She felt that his gaze was directed to the gentle swell of her breasts above the low-cut neckline of her blouse. He was very much a man and wasn't she inviting his sensuality to stir with her unconventional behaviour? Desire quickened within her for his touch, his kiss, his lean body against her own in the intimacy of passion.

She slid her fingers along the wooden rail until they touched his hand. He took them into a warm and reassuring clasp. Perhaps it wasn't a lover's eager welcoming, but at least it wasn't a rebuff, she thought gratefully.

She was so lovely, so appealing. Morgan bent his head and kissed her, so lightly that it was scarcely a kiss at all. Both resisted the temptation to let their lips linger, warm, cling in sudden need.

Heart thudding, body tingling in eager and excited

anticipation, Olivia said softly: 'I'd like to go now, Morgan . . .'

It was only a short drive to his flat but it seemed a never-ending journey to Olivia. It was alarming and disappointing that he seemed so remote, nothing like the lover that she was longing for him to be. Perhaps he had recoiled from her too-blatant eagerness. Perhaps, like every man, he preferred to be hunter rather than hunted, she thought bleakly.

Olivia didn't realise that her own silence, her own tension, indicated that she was nervous and distrustful of him despite the unexpected and rather surprising request for sanctuary. He determined that she shouldn't have cause to feel that he had taken the slightest advantage of her inclination to look upon him as a friend rather than a lover.

Arrived at the flat, he carried her case into the small guest room next to his own. 'You should be comfortable in here,' he said lightly, matter-of-fact. 'If you need anything you'll know where to find me, of course.'

Olivia was disconcerted. But she could scarcely point out that she had been hoping and longing to share his bed!

'Thank you,' she said carefully, doing her best to conceal flooding dismay and disappointment. 'It's really very good of you to take me in like this without a word of explanation.' She smiled at him gratefully. 'You haven't asked any questions. Aren't you curious?'

Not when the answers were all too obvious, he thought wryly, having noticed that she had said very little about Tom Knight and didn't want to be drawn into discussion of the man.

He shrugged. 'I think I expected you to dislike a

difficult situation. And I daresay your cousin made it obvious that you were an unnecessary third. Selfish people can be very insensitive.'

'She doesn't know that I'm with you, of course,' Olivia said quietly. 'In fact, I didn't actually tell her that I was leaving.'

He raised an eyebrow. 'I hope that Jean-Paul won't get the credit this time,' he said lightly.

Olivia suddenly remembered that she had asked Jean-Paul and Madeleine to come in for drinks that evening. It had gone right out of her mind. Well, it was much too late to do anything about it and she probably hadn't been missed.

She laughed, shook her head. 'Oh, she'll have learned by now that he's no longer interested in me,' she returned airily. 'I suppose you know that he's back . . . with a very pretty girl-friend?'

'The dancer. I met them in the village,' he agreed. 'She isn't as pretty as you are, Olivia.' He moved towards the door, resisting the irresistible temptation of her femininity with its tantalising reminder of another night when she had been warm and yielding and generous. Tonight, she was very much on the defensive, he sensed. 'Make yourself at home,' he invited easily. 'I shall be about for some time but don't let me disturb you. I have some papers to go through.'

As the door closed, Olivia sank to the edge of the bed, feeling quite desperate. This was not the way she had expected or wanted the evening to end! It hurt to be kept so pointedly at arms' length when she had tried so hard to be encouraging without exactly hurling herself into his arms!

She ached for his kiss and longed for the wonderful

world of delight to be found in his arms. How could he not know it! How could he turn away in cold indifference when he must sense her love and longing, her fierce need of him!

She struggled with the twin devils of pride and passion. Her body clamoured for him but she naturally shrank from the dreaded humiliation of a rejection. Loving him, why couldn't she just go to him and say so, she thought impulsively. Loving him, she knew she couldn't bear to see the sympathy and regret in the dark eyes because she couldn't stir him to loving and longing in return.

She opened her case and took out the things she would need for the night, knowing that she must make other plans for her future the very next day. Prepared to be Morgan's lover, she didn't intend to stay as his guest, she told herself proudly. At this hour, it was too late to return to the Villa Paradis and too late to book into a hotel. She had no reason to run away from Morgan, anyway—and she had no reason to stay, she thought bleakly.

She looked at the cold, uninviting bed and doubted that she would sleep while mind and heart and body were much too conscious of the man in the next room. She undressed, slowly and reluctantly, hearing the small sounds of movement about the flat with a desolate heart, remembering every magic moment of the other night she had spent beneath this roof and in his arms.

She drew the ribbon from her curls and they tumbled about her small face in bright confusion. She was about to run a brush through them before climbing into the narrow bed when a low knock took her flying to the door without a thought for pride or anything else.

She opened it, looked up at him, eyes wide and luminous with longing. Morgan's unsure heart contracted at the sight of that pretty, eager face. The words he had so carefully prepared and rehearsed were instantly forgotten. He put a tender hand to her head, twining his fingers among the soft curls, and drew her towards him, saying her name on an aching murmur of need.

He kissed her, very gently, not daring to draw her close for he knew that the throb of his body must betray him.

Olivia was filled from head to toe with thanksgiving. As he raised his head from that light but meaningful kiss, she melted against him. 'Hold me,' she said with tense longing. 'Just hold me . . .' It could never be enough but it was so much better than nothing at all!

He felt the merest whisper of her lips on his cheek, the soft sigh of her breath, and his arms went about her swiftly with sudden hunger. His body was on fire. His heart was so full of love and longing that it threatened to overflow into words that she might not welcome but must surely believe.

He abruptly realised that she was wearing nothing but the thin silk negligee. The teasing sensuality of her soft breasts thrusting against the flimsy stuff and the promise of enchantment in the lovely curves of her slender and wholly yielding body caused sexual excitement to mount in him rapidly to almost unbearable heights.

Olivia's arms stole about his neck. Loving him, wanting him, she pressed her body against him on a little moan of longing that told him that she was just as consumed by the fierçe flame of desire. Without rhyme or reason, they ignited each other to white heat at a touch. Nothing seemed to matter in that moment but the fierce, throbbing need for the ecstasy that each could give to the other. The world might come to an end, but it was doubtful if either would notice for they stood trembling on the brink of the magical world that belonged to lovers.

On a kiss, Morgan lifted her gently into his arms. She clung to him thankfully as he carried her to his room and his bed. There, he made slow and passion-charged love to her with lips and hands and ardent body until she was one glow of molten flame. They reached the highest peaks of ecstasy in mutual and glorious triumph such as few lovers knew this side of heaven and Olivia came slowly and reluctantly back to reality in the warm and comforting security of his embrace.

I love you, he had told her on the crest of that mountainous tidal wave of passion.

I love you, she had murmured in soft and sighing response as he swept her with him to those magnificent heights.

Now, both wondered if the words had been really meant or were merely born of the moment's exultant delight. Both desperately hoped that they were true for the sake of a very necessary happiness and peace of mind. Both were silent, neither daring to break the lingering spell of enchantment.

Clasped in his arms, floating on a tide of golden content, Olivia kissed the warm, slightly salt flesh of his muscular shoulder. She traced the sensual, faintly smiling mouth with her fingers in light, loving caress. His smile deepened. He drew her even closer in the tenderness of loving.

'Lovely Olivia,' he murmured, very low. '*Darling* . . .' He kissed her hair, her temple, her curving eyelids, her soft cheek as he traced a slow and sensuous route to her warmly responsive mouth.

She kissed him, heart on her lips.

Morgan's heart leaped. This was the Olivia he had known and loved since time began. This was the Olivia he had found and thought lost, and found again. This was his love, his life, his dearest girl—and if he was the luckiest man in the whole wide world, she loved and needed him, too!

He raised himself on an elbow to look into the lovely grey eyes. 'Olivia,' he said, her name a very special endearment on his lips. He brushed a strand of hair from her face and bent to kiss her, very tenderly. 'Oh, Olivia,' he said again, soft and almost breathless with love and longing and the wonder of knowing this warm and enchanting girl. 'I . . .'

The telephone rang, shattering the moment.

Morgan tensed and the words of love died on his lips.

Olivia sensed the sudden and frustrating change of mood. She sighed and drew herself gently from his arms, knowing that a doctor couldn't ignore a summons, night or day.

The telephone continued to make its shrill sound, insistent. Morgan cursed beneath his breath, smiled at her wryly and rolled over to lift the receiver from its cradle.

Olivia recognised the swift transition from lover to doctor as he listened to the disembodied voice on the other end of the line. She saw him tense and he fired some questions in rapid, soft-spoken French of which she only caught a few words. But they were enough.

That sixth sense suddenly went into action and an icy finger of fear trailed its way down her spine. She knew even before he turned to her with a very tender concern in his dark eyes.

'Celeste . . .' she said quietly.

Morgan nodded. 'She's taken an overdose of sleeping pills.'

CHAPTER THIRTEEN

IT was not just a half-hearted bid for attention or even a desperate cry for help as Olivia had hoped. It was a determined attempt at suicide. Celeste had been drinking steadily for most of the evening and then taken a handful of sleeping tablets when she went to her room. Fortunately, Tom had been uneasy and had walked in to catch her with the bottle of pills in her hand.

Waiting for the ambulance, he had marched her up and down the room, forcibly keeping her awake by talking to her and insisting on answers, shaking her roughly whenever she threatened to slump in his arms. The bruises on her upper arms and shoulders bore witness to his rough but necessary handling.

Arrived at the clinic, she underwent all the indignity of a stomach wash-out. Tom insisted on staying with her, holding her hand, comforting and reassuring even though Celeste scarcely seemed to know that he was there. Perhaps he felt guilty. Perhaps he had been shocked into an awareness of her very real dependence on him and a sense of responsibility towards the wife he had never loved. But he was genuinely concerned and distressed.

Celeste seemed to rally. Everyone began to breathe again. Then, suddenly, she slipped into coma. For some hours, it was touch and go whether she lived. It was not possible to be sure just how much poison had been absorbed by her system.

There was nothing that Tom could do but wait and worry while Morgan and his efficient team did all they could. Throughout the night, Celeste was in a side ward in the small but progressively-equipped Intensive Care Unit, an intravenous drip supplying her with vital fluids, heartbeat and respiration being automatically monitored by machines.

Needing to dress in a hurry to accompany Morgan to the main building, Olivia had instinctively taken her Kit's uniform from her case. In the mauve frock and with her Kit's badge pinned carefully to the collar, she felt that she had a right to be present while Morgan fought for her cousin's life.

Putting on her uniform meant that she also put on a very necessary detachment despite her concern and the dreadful weight of guilt about her heart.

Olivia felt that she was very much to blame. If she hadn't rushed away from the Villa Paradis in such haste to be with Morgan that evening such a terrible thing couldn't have happened, she told herself heavily.

She would have noticed and taken steps to stop Celeste from drinking too much. She would have recognised the signs of suicidal depression in good time. Most important of all, Celeste wouldn't have had access to the sleeping pills in the leather drugs case that Olivia had foolishly forgotten to bring away with her, mind too full of her own selfish concerns.

She realised that she had been too easily reassured about Celeste's frame of mind because she was so anxious that her plans shouldn't misfire. She had used Tom's attempt to make love to her as a springboard for her own desires, she thought with regret, knowing that she had leaped into Morgan's arms and into his bed with a wanton disregard for her patient and everything else.

She was a disgrace to her uniform and her badge. She had put herself before her patient. She had failed Celeste—*and* Morgan who had trusted her to keep a careful eye on Celeste. She had lain in his arms and delighted in his lovemaking while her cousin, feeling herself to be unloved and unwanted by the man who meant everything to her, had quietly set about taking her own life.

In retrospect, Olivia could conjure up several small but meaningful cameos of the previous evening that ought to have warned her of the danger in leaving Celeste with only Tom who didn't seem to know or care that she was so desperately unhappy.

Remembering the bloom of radiance that had given her cousin an even greater beauty when she came from the clinic with Tom, Olivia didn't doubt that something had shattered that newfound confidence in the future. It seemed only too likely that Celeste had known of Tom's badly-timed and ill-judged approaches to Olivia. The delicate balance of her mind had been sufficiently disturbed for her to feel that she had nothing left to live for—and Olivia was ready to blame herself in a hundred ways.

It must be her fault that Tom had fallen in love with her and continued to love her—and therefore also her fault that her cousin's marriage had been doomed from the beginning. It must be her fault that Celeste had clung to straws throughout the weeks of despair. She should have forced her to face facts and come to terms with life without Tom. It must be her fault that Tom had reluctantly resumed the rôle of husband and made promises that he knew he couldn't keep. Perhaps she should have sent him away and encouraged Celeste to find new happiness with Morgan who was so caring and so concerned, so obviously willing her to live throughout the long night.

Certainly it was her fault that she hadn't left the Villa Paradis as soon as Tom decided to stay in her cousin's absence. Heaven knew what Celeste had imagined to have gone on between them once she realised that Tom was in love with her, Olivia thought ruefully. To Celeste, it must have seemed that in one fell swoop she had not only lost her husband once more but also the affection and loyalty and support of her cousin, so precious to her. No wonder she had wanted to die!

But she wasn't going to die.

Olivia was flooded with relief as she saw the sudden draining of tension from Morgan's tall frame. He straightened from his examination of Celeste's pupils and smiled at her across the bed. 'She'll do,' he said quietly, using the traditional term for patients who were expected to make a full recovery.

Olivia put a hand to her suddenly quivering mouth and tears lurched on to her long lashes. 'Oh, thank God . . . !' she said emotionally.

Morgan moved to her side. He put an arm about the shaking shoulders. 'Cry, love,' he said gently, gathering her close, knowing something of the turmoil of her heart and mind. 'You've been very brave . . .'

Morgan had learned a great deal about Olivia that night. In the early hours, he had talked to Knight. The man had been under stress and consumed with a guilt that found relief in a torrent of self-accusation. Morgan knew that a doctor's ear was often a confessional for the sick or anxious or distressed and he had resigned himself to listening when every instinct urged him to walk away.

He had learned of Knight's long-felt passion for Olivia and her refusal to encourage it and the subsequent frustration and despair that had vented itself on the wife who loved him.

He had learned of Knight's effort to forget Olivia in the arms of another woman and its failure, the desperate need that had brought him to the South of France in search of her, the subsequent decision to give up hoping and try to make something of his marriage.

He had learned that Celeste had inadvertently witnessed one last attempt on Knight's part to persuade Olivia to go away with him. As soon as they were alone that evening, she had accused them of being in love and wanting her out of the way—and he hadn't denied it. This was the result!

Everything that Morgan had been told had seemed to bear out his own construction of the way things were between Olivia and Tom Knight. He had been stirred to admiration and respect for her integrity, her loyalty to Celeste, her continued refusal to take her own happiness at the expense of someone else. It helped to know that she was all the things he had believed, all the things he had loved.

He held her very tenderly. Loving her and needing her, he knew that he had no claim to her, no right to ask that she put Knight out of her life, no hope of marrying her. It was rather ironic that a Kit's nurse had turned him into a confirmed bachelor with her proven lack of love or trust and that another Kit's nurse had reversed his way of thinking all in a moment with her warm and generous heart. If only he had known and loved Olivia in those days when he was a registrar and she was a first-year nurse . . .

In his arms, Olivia broke down and cried, not only for Celeste who had been brought back to a world that she didn't want to face, but also for her own shortcomings.

Falling in love had seemed to be the most important thing in the world. Wanting Morgan, she had sacrificed pride, self-respect, loyalty and the strong sense of duty that had been instilled in her during the years of training at a famous hospital. Her behaviour had almost caused the death of a patient. She just wasn't fit to wear the highly-prized badge of a Kit's nurse! It wasn't likely that Morgan would wish her to work with him at the clinic now that she had proved to be so unreliable!

Now, he held her and comforted her and didn't speak a single word of condemnation but she was sure that he could have nothing but contempt for her. He couldn't despise her more than she despised herself, she thought heavily, drawing away and struggling with the tears that couldn't wash away the guilt and remorse and heartache.

'Someone should tell Tom . . .' she said stiffly.

'Yes, of course.' Morgan went out of the side ward. Tom Knight was slumped in a chair in the corridor, heavy-eyed and despondent. He was on his feet in an instant at Morgan's approach, anxious and apprehensive, expecting the worst.

Morgan put a hand on the man's shoulder, reassuring.

'She's sleeping,' he said quietly. 'She's going to be all right. You can go in now.'

He saw that the man paused as he went into the small room. For a long moment, he looked at Olivia. She looked back at him without so much as the flicker of a smile, any kind of feeling. Morgan admired her strength of mind . . . and he felt a stirring of sympathy for Knight. A man couldn't love or not love to order. He knew how *he* felt about Olivia and how much he longed for her to love him, need him.

Olivia turned away from Knight. He went to the bed and put his hand to Celeste's fine-drawn and almost transparently pale face, whether to confirm for himself that she lived or on a sudden rush of tender regret only he knew.

Olivia came out into the corridor and closed the door on husband and wife. Heaven knew what the outcome would be, but Celeste was going to need careful handling and a great deal of attention in the weeks to come. She didn't feel that Tom cared enough to cope. But she knew that it wouldn't be her responsibility. Celeste would never trust her again, obviously. And she didn't want to be within a hundred miles of Tom Knight!

'There's nothing more we can do here for the moment,' Morgan said firmly, taking her arm. 'I suggest breakfast and then bed. You'll feel better when you've had some sleep, Olivia.'

She didn't argue. They left the clinic together and crossed the wide lawns to the rambling old house and his flat. She didn't mean to stay, of course. He was being kind, but she didn't think he wanted her to stay. For her part, there was no magic any more in being with him, she thought unhappily. She could never lie in his arms again without remembering that her passion for him had almost cost Celeste her life.

She was tired and emotional. Her heart was very heavy and the future seemed bleak. She didn't know what she was going to do or where she could go. Kit's had been her home for four years until she had answered her cousin's cry for help.

Kit's. Olivia unpinned her badge from her collar and looked at it, turned it over and over in her fingers, remembering. She had been a good nurse. She had loved her job and cared about her patients. She had been efficient and reliable and responsible. People had trusted her. Celeste had trusted her. She had let everyone down, including herself.

She sighed.

'What's that?' Morgan placed mugs of steaming coffee on the low table. Olivia looked up, roused from reverie. 'What are you holding?' She opened her hand and showed him the silver badge and then slipped it into the pocket of her uniform frock. He smiled at her, very warm. 'That badge means a lot to you, doesn't it? Three years of blood, sweat and tears—and dodging irate Sisters! It's a large lump out of anyone's life.'

She nodded, not trusting herself to speak. His kindness, his sympathy, were almost too much for her self-control. She didn't want him to be nice to her. It only made her realise just why she loved him and how much she loved him and how dreadful it would be not to see him any more. Her chin wobbled. Hastily she reached for the coffee and carried the mug to her lips to hide the childish lack of control. Tears weren't going to solve anything, she told herself sternly.

Morgan leaned back in his chair, said quietly: 'I mean to recommend a course of pyschiatric treatment for your cousin. She's very highly-strung and she's been through a very difficult time. It needed only one small push to take her over the edge and into a complete breakdown. She was riding too high during the last few days and I didn't approve of her leaving the clinic just yet, as you know. I had reservations about the too-sudden reconciliation between her and Knight, too,' he added carefully, feeling that he touched on dangerous ground. 'I just didn't feel that she was in very good hands, I'm afraid.'

'He doesn't care about her at all,' she said stonily, wondering what would happen in the future. It didn't seem likely that Tom and Celeste would stay married after all that had happened. One day, she might be free to find lasting happiness and real security with someone else. Olivia wondered unhappily if that someone else would prove to be Morgan.

He hesitated. 'That was my impression, I must admit.'

'Celeste has refused to face facts all these weeks. Then she just couldn't cope when the truth was forced on her.' Olivia bit her lip, went on: 'I don't know, but I imagine they quarrelled. They are both quick-tempered. Tom didn't really want to stay married to her and I expect he said so without pulling any punches. He wouldn't care how much he hurt her.'

Morgan ran his hands over his dark hair. 'Knight told me something of the situation.' He smiled wryly. 'Doctors have these confidences thrust on them. Very often, we are told far more than we wish to know.'

Olivia glanced at him, alert. His tone was fractionally too kind. 'Did he . . . mention me?'

He leaned forward and captured her slender hands. 'He could scarcely *not* mention you,' he said gently. 'But you've nothing to regret, Olivia. You have been a very good friend to your cousin, I believe.'

'Friend!' She was suddenly bitter. 'How can you think so!'

'You're not to blame for what happened,' he told her firmly. 'You couldn't have prevented it.'

'The pills,' she said flatly. 'I left them behind. I am to blame.'

'You couldn't have known what would happen!'

'But I *did* know! She was unhappy, withdrawn. It was obvious that something was very wrong. I just didn't want to *see*, Morgan. I was being selfish. I just wanted . . .' She broke off. He couldn't wish to know that she had wanted so much to be with him that nothing else had mattered.

'To escape?' Morgan smiled at her in warm understanding. 'I know it hasn't been easy for you. I don't think you've been selfish or negligent, Olivia. It's almost possible that you've sacrificed too much for Celeste. Certainly no one could have done more for her!'

She shook her head. 'I knew she was unstable, not to be trusted with drugs. You don't have to be kind, Morgan. It *is* my fault!'

He looked at the white, tense face, the weariness-smudged eyes. 'You're tired and things are out of perspective,' he said lightly. 'Celeste is going to be fine. I'm more concerned about you—and I'm not just being kind!' He rose and drew her from the chair, kissed her lightly on the brow. 'Let's get you to bed, darling . . .'

Bemused and bewildered, Olivia allowed him to undress her like a child and lift her into the wide bed and draw the covers about her with tender hands. He closed the curtains to shut out the morning sun. Watching him, she felt that he was the kindest, most caring man in the world and her heart swelled with love for him.

Despite everything, he could still be good to her and she was grateful for the smallest sign of a lingering liking and affection. She couldn't bear to think what her life was going to be like without him. She had found heaven in his arms. She knew that hell was a world without Morgan.

She tasted the salt on her lips before she knew that tears were streaming down her cheeks. She turned her face into the pillow, stifling a sob . . . and then he was beside her, sliding his arms about her, his body warm and comforting against her own. He held her without passion, his lips against her hair and tenderness rather than fire in his embrace. As always, he knew and supplied a need and she loved him for that unfailing sensitivity. This is what it would be like to be his wife, to spend the rest of her life with him, she thought wistfully, knowing it would never be.

The heavy thud of his heart was reassuring. The clasp of his arms was comforting. It was tempting to imagine that he loved her and needed her and would never let her go . . . and on that soothing fancy, she relaxed and drifted into sleep.

The soft sigh of her breath told Morgan that she slept. He touched his lips to her bright hair, loving her, needing her, hoping that he had eased some of her heartache.

He wondered what the future held for them. Some instinct told him that she would never go to Knight, come what may. She might love him but she wouldn't trust him with her happiness, Morgan suspected. He hoped with all his heart that she would stay in France, near to him. He would be anything that she wanted, he vowed . . . friend, confidant, companion. Lover, too, if she needed him. She had become very dear, very precious, very necessary to him.

He intended to stay awake and savour the delight of holding her to his heart. But he was lulled into sleep before he knew it by the warmth of her body and the rhythmic murmur of her breathing.

He woke to the sharpness of hunger and an appetising aroma. He leaped out of bed and snatched up a robe and went to the kitchen.

Olivia turned from the cooker. 'Good morning,' she greeted him, smiling. 'I hope you fancy bacon and eggs. I couldn't find anything else.'

She had woken with his arms still about her and an unaccountable happiness about her heart. She didn't know if they had a future, if he would ever really love her. But she couldn't help feeling that the undeniable rapport between them, the closeness and the understanding that could transcend the physical delight in each other, counted for more than Celeste's appealing loveliness. Men might dream about women like Celeste with her fragile and delicate beauty. They settled for the reality of women like herself, very often . . .

Morgan's heart contracted as he looked down at her. She was so pretty, so sweet, so appealing. He loved her so much. It was time that she knew it, he decided. A man had to try for his happiness when it was within his reach, after all. There was something in the way she smiled at him that quickened his heart with sudden hope.

He reached for her, kissed her, lightly but with a hint of lingering. 'I fancy *you*,' he said softly, teasing, an ardent glow smouldering in the depths of his dark eyes. 'Where have you been all my life, lovely Olivia?'

Her name was an unmistakable endearment on his lips. Her heart lifted at the warm tenderness in his eyes. She smiled at him with love. 'Learning to cook bacon and eggs to perfection—and I won't allow them to spoil!' she said firmly, moving out of his arms.

'Learning to be indispensable in lots of other ways, too,' he said lightly, watching as she deftly transferred the hot food to well-warmed plates. 'A man could get used to having you around.'

Olivia sat down at the table with him and poured coffee into the waiting cups. 'That sounds like an invitation,' she said carefully, smiling. 'I might be tempted to take you up on it . . .'

He looked at her thoughtfully. 'It isn't an invitation, Olivia. It's a proposal. I'm asking you to marry me . . . very clumsily, I must admit.'

Olivia's heart rocked. Shock and soaring delight shivered down the length of her spine and the unexpected words tumbled about in her head in echoing confusion. 'You really want to marry me?' she stumbled incredulously.

He leaned to touch his lips to her bright curls. 'Very much.'

She searched his dark eyes, still not believing. 'But Celeste . . .'

'Celeste will have to manage without you,' he interrupted, very firm. 'There's always someone to take care of the Celestes of this world, darling. Ever since I met you, I've wanted to take care of you, make you happy.' He laid his strong hand along her cheek in a loving caress. 'I love you very much . . .'

Bacon and eggs, cooked to perfection, were completely forgotten as she went into his arms on an impulsive murmur of love. As their lips met and he knew again the generous warmth of her giving in the way she melted into his embrace, Morgan was grateful for the destiny that had brought this lovely Kit's nurse so unexpectedly into his life.

And Olivia's heart was very full. One night of love had changed her whole life and brought her the promise of a happiness that only he could fulfil . . .